AF439056

Christmas Dancing Genes

BY
D.T. Everly

© 2026 Little Studio Films

All rights reserved.
No part of this book may be reproduced or transmitted in any form or by any means, including graphics, electronic, or mechanical, including photocopying, recording, taping, or by any information storage or retrieval system, without the permission in writing from the author and publisher.

Published by Little Studio Films

ISBN: 979-8-9957353-1-1
LCCN: 2026910635

Edited by: Heidi Stangeland
Cover by: Heidi Stangeland

DEDICATION

To my husband, my greatest supporter who fills my life with love, laughter and strength. Thank you for standing beside me for every chapter, both written and lived.

To our two dogs, whose wagging tails, gentle hearts, and endless devotion remind me daily of life's simplest joys.

And for our son, who we haven't met yet, but already love beyond words. You are a quiet presence, a heartbeat, a future waiting to unfold. This book was written in the space between who I was and who I am becoming because of you. In the waiting, the wondering, the dreaming of your face, I found new meaning in every page.

TABLE OF CONTENTS

Chapter 1: Charisse

January 1997

"Enough! Stop!" Charisse screamed. She was disoriented and awake on an operating table at New Life Fertility Clinic—a notable facility located in Scottsdale, Arizona.

To the doctor's astonishment, Charisse had awakened in the middle of her egg retrieval procedure. The anesthesiologist quickly replenished her painkillers and anesthesia. The horrified medical assistant instructed Charisse to go back to sleep. Slightly confused and lightheaded, Charisse wearily closed her eyes, and everything went dark again.

Thirty minutes later, Charisse woke up in pain, and the first thing the medical assistant blurted out was, "That was funny when you woke up in the middle of the procedure!"

There was nothing funny about it, Charisse thought as her heart pounded murderously. She was practically rushed out of the clinic after the procedure. Thankfully, her best friend was waiting for her outside the office. Charisse overheard the reproductive endocrinologist,

Dr. Daniel Marker, sulk that he was going to be late for his tee time that afternoon. *Whoa! Those painkillers must be kicking in,* Charisse realized as she effortlessly drifted off into a dreamlike state.

November 1996

Charisse Gardiner, a blisteringly beautiful young woman with hazel eyes and long, brunette hair, arrived home and stumbled into her apartment after a night of dancing. At the tender age of twenty-five, she lived alone in an apartment in Scottdale, Arizona, a renowned college town, and the only home she'd known since leaving New York as a teenager. It was the first time that she had lived anywhere without roommates and Charisse was trying to make it as an adult college graduate without having to move back home, as everyone predicted she would. She wanted to prove them all wrong, especially those townies who never left New York after high school. But she needed money to do it.

Since the age of five, Charisse had been an exceptionally talented dancer. Her mother, Sherry, enrolled little Charisse in tap, jazz, and ballet classes, and she never stopped dancing.

The only thing Charisse loved more than dancing? Christmas! Since living in Arizona didn't always encourage the holiday spirit, Charisse overcompensated by decking out every inch of her apartment with Christmas lights, stockings, and decorations, starting in October. There was something magical about Christmastime that made her forget she was alone. She had a resounding apathy for all other aspects of life.

Charisse didn't have the bandwidth to arrange dates, buy new outfits, or go to the nail salon. She would rather stay at home and watch Christmas movies. It didn't matter what time of the year it was. Christmas always made everything better. It did sometimes make her wish she were living within a Christmas movie instead of starring in her own life. She kept her fake, white tabletop Christmas tree out all year long. The colorful ornaments blended well with any theme.

Charisse had been preparing for her appointment at New Life Fertility Clinic in Scottsdale. It was only a 45-minute drive from her apartment. Charisse had spent the better part of the past year researching fertility centers in the area, choosing where to donate her eggs. It was a decision she made after pledging to do something selfless that holiday season. Little did she realize at the time how it would impact the rest of her life, starting with an impromptu move to New York City to pursue her lifelong dream of becoming a professional dancer.

Chapter 2: Amelia

December 2022

Amelia hailed a cab just in time to make it to class, as she could no longer walk through the streets. The sky was painted red as if it were a canvas of the heavens. High wind was blowing out of the northwest, and the cold air was coming in from Canada. Her right shoulder ached as she was carrying her brown Australian puppy, Ballare. It was a brisk winter day in New York, and she was thrilled to experience the change of seasons. Growing up in the southwest, the only winter she knew was during those few months when the temperatures dropped below eighty degrees during the day. Amelia had moved to New York City to pursue a graduate degree in social work at New York University. That is where she met her best friend, Frederick, a quintessential New York City guy born and bred, who had hair implants to cover up his progressing male pattern baldness that he inherited from his estranged father.

"It's about time girl! Next time don't wear stilettos to walk ten blocks!" exclaimed Frederick. Frederick was the human embodiment of the grandeur of New York City if there ever was one.

"Next time, I'm wearing Crocs!" joked Amelia. Frederick gasped in response.

"Crocs are making a comeback. You'd be surprised," Amelia said.

"Crocs are positively medieval!" Frederick protested.

"Quiet, you two in the back!" Professor Bryant shouted. They were his least favorite students, as he didn't think highly of gossiping during class. Professor Bryant's lectures sent most students into a deep sleep, and each sleep jolted their head awake at this change in tone from him.

"Look at this," Frederick softly whispered as he passed a flyer to Amelia. She grabbed it and read it thoroughly. It was for an open audition for dancers for the Times Square New Year's Eve Dance Special, judged by the renowned choreographer Charisse Gardiner. "Forget it!" Amelia loudly whispered and crumpled up the flier.

"Oh, come on! I saw the pictures. You were such a good dancer growing up. Plus, I can't do it without you. You're my best friend.

Please," Frederick begged.

"Then you can choose to do it. I am not choosing to. Plus, I am positively bedeviled with work," Amelia pleaded. "Life is full of things we don't choose," Frederick responded.

"Only if you treat me to my favorite Mocha Lattes order," Amelia negotiated. She continued, "One bag of green mint tea, one bag of Vermont green tea, a dash of cinnamon with steamed almond milk."

"Done!" Frederick agreed, laughing. His laugh sounded like a leaf blower. Amelia found it endearing.

Amelia hadn't danced or loved since her parents passed away years ago. Her memories of that time were rather nebulous. All her passion and love departed with her parents. When her parents were alive, the world seemed soft and filled with possibility. Amelia grew up as an only child in the wealthy town of Scottsdale, Arizona. For the most part, she had an easy life that most people would envy, until tragedy struck her family. Her parents were so loving and caring. When she lost them, she felt utterly alone in the world.

As a young girl, Amelia was given the choice to take up any hobby or sport she desired. Despite her parents' enthusiasm for her playing sports, Amelia was always compelled to spend her time dancing. Dancing was her passion. It came naturally to her.

After graduating college, Amelia needed to get out of Scottsdale and the state of Arizona. Amelia applied for and was accepted to a graduate social work program at New York University. It was a dream she had as teenager. When Amelia left for New York, the family estate lawyer, Jordana, had generously gifted Amelia an adorably brown mini–Australian Shepard puppy who Amelia named Ballare, meaning "to dance" in Italian.

Chapter 3: Patrick

December 2022

"Cheers to Patrick!" The family's voices cried in unison. Patrick's loud, Irish family was celebrating his upcoming adventure to New York City from their hometown of Boston. Patrick was a boisterous, gregarious, Bostonian to the core. "I just want to say how proud I am of you. You'll do great. I can't wait to see you on television on New Year's Eve! I'll miss you! And I always thought you were too good for Victoria," Patrick's mother, Kelly, concluded her toast. The family sat in silence for a minute.

Victoria was still a sensitive topic for Patrick, and everyone knew, except for his mother, Kelly. In preparing for this unchartered adventure, Patrick had assumed his college sweetheart, Victoria, would be enthusiastic about the move, and would want to come with him to New York. Life did not turn out the way Patrick had planned in this instance. Patrick's father, Declan, broke up the awkward silence by adding, "No matter what happens in NYC never stop wearing your Red Sox hat!" Patrick would never go a day without wearing his red baseball cap representing his favorite sports team.

Patrick, an aspiring entertainment lawyer from Boston, left his life in the Bay State to audition for the Times Square New Year's Eve Dance Special. Patrick was raised by an Irish American family in Boston. His father, Declan, was a Harvard-educated attorney, and his mother, a former professional dancer. Patrick's brother, Connor, followed in their father's footsteps, attending Harvard Law, and became a lawyer. Connor got a job at a commercial litigation law firm in downtown Boston using his father's connections. In contrast, Patrick graduated from Harvard law school and obtained a job at an entertainment law firm while studying for the bar exam. The one activity that bonded the family was attending Red Sox games.

Patrick delayed sending in his bar exam application until he eventually admitted to himself and his family that he wanted to pursue a dance career. He spent months blaming the delay on the laziness of state workers. Dancing had always been Patrick's true passion, but he didn't want to disappoint his father and brother. For years, instead of studying, he had been practicing dancing. He never needed to study.

He was a naturally proficient test-taker. As a result, he had more time to practice dancing. When he learned about the open audition for the Times Square New Year's Eve Dance Special, he knew this was his calling. Patrick instantly rented an apartment and booked a flight to New York city. His mother found out about the opportunity through an old friend, Charisse, who had choreographed her dances when she lived in New York. Patrick's mother went to college in New York City, and Patrick's family was nothing but supportive and loving, especially since his mother had a special connection to the city.

The same couldn't be said for Patrick's girlfriend, Victoria. As soon as he told her he would not be going to law school, she told him she no longer loved him, and that it was over. It appeared that Victoria was more in love with the idea of Patrick being a lawyer than Patrick as a person. She saw him as a collection of flaws. Shortly thereafter, Patrick embarked on his journey to New York city, solo. The statute of limitations for licking the wound of a broken heart had expired and Patrick needed to move on with his life, leaving behind his love and career. Patrick had always said nothing in life is as solid a state as it appears.

Patrick arrived in Manhattan on a brisk winter day. His plane landed at JFK and then he took a cab to a 600-square-foot studio in Midtown. As planned, he'd arrived in the big city a week before auditions to practice in the new environment. The next morning Patrick walked down the block to get a coffee at the local, trendy coffee shop. Crowds of people flew by him, speeding and bumping him on the shoulder as they passed. There seemed to be loud construction projects on every corner. Patrick thought how this city couldn't be more different than Boston.

Although most would consider Boston a large metropolis, the locals knew it had much more of a small-town feel. There was something about the vibe in New York that inspired Patrick to want to be the best and gave him that extra push of motivation. He spent the next few days practicing dance routines in his tiny, temporary apartment. He knew this was his chance to prove to himself and his family that he had made the right decision. At times, though, a wave of sadness enveloped Patrick, when he realized he was alone in New York, and that Victoria wasn't there to cheer him on and motivate him.

Patrick ensured that his rental was right down the street from a trendy coffee shop, Mocha Lattes. As a lawyer, Patrick pounded two cups of coffee before he put a bite of food in his mouth. In fact, he purchased the coffee maker that still sits in the lounge of his old law firm. There was no time for trendy coffee shops while practicing the law. However, since he was in New York City and pursuing his dream, Patrick was happy to treat himself. He embraced the change in pace. Patrick walked into the coffee shop and immediately laid eyes on the most radiant, beguiling woman he had ever seen in his life. His eyes were like a yoyo looking up and down at her.

Distracted by her beauty, Patrick stubbed his toe against the leg of a chair and a single tear dripped down his left eye as he suffered in silence to conceal his public embarrassment. Her lavender scent floated out to Patrick. The fleeting toe pain wasn't enough to snap him out of his trance. The captivating woman had hazel eyes and brunette, wavy hair that flowed past her shoulders and whisked her elbows. Patrick noticed a tiny clip placed on the right side of her head that pulled her hair back ever so slightly and gave off an effortless beauty vibe, the kind that only a woman who doesn't have to try gives off. The kind of woman who has been beautiful her entire life and always had it easy, who didn't have to spend hours in the bathroom every morning getting ready.

The mystery woman was wearing all black athleisure leggings, zip up jacket and matching sneakers. Ever since he was younger, Patrick's eyes involuntarily twitched when he saw a female who he was attracted to for the first time and the biological twitch never applied to a situation as it did on that day.

The woman grabbed her green tea to go and walked past Patrick on her way out of the coffee shop. Patrick was so focused on the woman's smile, that he didn't notice the brown, fluffy, toy-sized Mini Australian Shepard puppy in her gym bag until he heard something yapping. The captivating beauty of the woman and adorable puppy clouded his ability to think. The puppy had hazel eyes that closely matched the beautiful woman's own eyes. The curious, fluffy, brown face popped out of the gym bag and Patrick nervously put his hand out to pet the puppy. "Ouch!" Patrick screamed at the puppy, but his finger and blood began to pour out of him. The coffee in his other hand spilled and droplets hit the woman, who was obviously fastidious about keeping her clothes unstained. The pain was too severe to suffer in silence this time and Patrick effortlessly made a storm with his eyes. The woman observed him bemused, as if she were watching an animal do something unexpected: a dog wearing a bow tie while playing the saxophone. Thereupon, a disproportional rage came over her. "Next time keep your hands out of my bag!" The woman gave a look that could kill and just like that, she was gone. Patrick was thunderstruck.

Chapter 4: Mocha Lattes

Patrick eagerly left his apartment the next day to attend the first day of auditions after brushing his teeth five times and fixing his hair ten times. He must've blinked 1000 times and pinched himself to ensure that it wasn't all a dream. It clearly wasn't he reminded himself, as his finger had a band aid with dried blood from the dog bite and his toe was still throbbing. "Yup, not a dream," Patrick whispered to himself.

Patrick walked through the wild, crowed streets of Manhattan. He overheard the quintessential blowharding between corporate Wall Street guys. Patrick bumped into a group of people as he read graffiti on a wall which spelled out the sentence, "It's lonely at the top." Something about the energy in Manhattan was in direct contrast to the streets of downtown Boston. Patrick felt freer to let loose and even more confident. Patrick couldn't help but feel overly optimistic that things were finally going his way.

"Welcome all, I am one of the judges, Charisse Gardiner," Charisse announced. "Any relation to Isabella Stewart Gardiner?" Patrick asked, referencing once of the most famous Bostonian women in history and whose name is on the museum at the center of one of the biggest art heists in world history. "No?" responded Charisse, incredulously. Patrick evidently didn't read the room and clearly was not in Boston anymore.

"Nice to meet you," Amelia stated as she put her hand out for a handshake, but Patrick awkwardly stood there with his hand down as he was distracted by the scent of her sweet perfume and then embarrassment suddenly enveloped him. She continued, "And for what it's worth, like Isabella Stewart Gardner, I often let me wit run ahead of my grace." Patrick instantly recognized the woman he spotted in the coffee shop the day before. He was dumbfounded by the witty reference. But he quickly amended himself. "My apologies. The pleasure is mine," he said, and put his hand out, hoping the awkward moment would quickly be forgotten. Patrick dropped his gaze, as she was too pretty to look at him directly. *Hot plus tall means he'll be completely insufferable,* Amelia thought to herself. The vision of Amelia miraculously caused the memory of Victoria to begin to fade. Amelia's face was frozen, and it was at that point he realized that she recognized him as well. As if the moment couldn't get any more awkward, Patrick's eyes began to blink uncontrollably. "Hey, all things considered, I think I owe you a coffee. It's on me if you'd like to meet at that coffee shop tomorrow morning before practice," he nervously added, trying to salvage the moment.

"I don't do coffee, but appreciate the offer," Amelia replied as she rolled her eyes.

"It's impossible to please a woman," Patrick whispered to himself.

Patrick had swiftly upgraded from nuisance to adversary and finally to partner to Amelia.

Amelia was never able to drink coffee. Ever since she was a little girl, Amelia had an unexplained allergy to dairy. "And who drinks coffee without dairy?" She used to question people who wondered how she could function without coffee. For the first few years of Amelia's life, doctors had incorrectly labeled her as a fussy child because of her refusal to drink milk. It wasn't until elementary school that Amelia was officially diagnosed with the allergy. She always felt left out when she heard the milk lady's cart rolling towards her classroom with small cartons of chocolate milk. Since she wasn't able to stomach the taste of dairy free milk options, Amelia just accepted the fact that she would never be a coffee person. Instead, she opted for a life of drinking green tea.

"You're missing out," Patrick said, as if he could read her thoughts. He winked at Amelia and walked away without saying another word. He was supremely adept at embodying confidence to hide insecurity.

"Leave it to men to be so insensitive and crass," Amelia whispered to herself ever so softly. She was a natural contrarian.

Chapter 5: Frederick

Thanks to Frederick, Amelia came to realize that her childhood dream was not dead and gone. As kawaii as Patrick was, Amelia knew she did not need any distractions if she was serious about advancing her career and following her newly revived dream. She came to New York City laser focused on one thing: becoming a social worker. Her real, lifelong dream of becoming a professional dancer had been left on the backburner for too long. This competition was the best opportunity to cross her path since moving to New York, and she did not want to let it pass her by. Love was not on the menu for Amelia. How was she going to juggle the tail end of her college semester at NYU and dance auditions for the opportunity of a lifetime? "I'll just wing it," she responded to Frederick's inquiry and just like that, she reluctantly agreed to follow her once extinct dream of becoming a professional dancer. Frederick was an old soul, a curmudgeon, a misanthrope, in a young man's body.

Frederick, always impressed by Amelia's tenacity to tackle life's toughest challenges with grace, replied, "And that's why you are my spirit animal." Amelia winked and responded, "And you, mine." "So, tell me, what was the awkward moment all about with your stud of a partner?" Frederick asked. "He's coffee shop guy! The one my little Ballare bit that I told you about last night. "Coffee shop guy is handsome! Not at all what I imagined!" Frederick squealed. "I didn't notice. I'm laser focused on the audition," Amelia objected. "You know, you do have to work with him." You might want to reconsider drinking coffee," Frederick said as he winked. "I will not be drinking coffee anytime soon. Ballare is a good judge of character, and I trust her," Amelia replied. "Ballare is just a dog, despite you referring to him as a puppy still after all this time!" Frederick exclaimed. "You know Ballare was a rescue from the estate lawyer that she gave me after my parents passed away. She was alone and I was sad. She is my only family now," Amelia responded. "Don't forget. We are family too," Frederick replied.

Amelia, tearing up a bit, declared, "Life's going to be easy for us someday. It must. Someday I'll be perfect enough to be loved by an actual human being, not just an animal." Frederick started to tear up as well. They quietly sat there, on their east village dormitory rooftop, enjoying the most underrated view of the city that never sleeps.

From the outside looking in, Frederick's life appeared to be privileged and his family the embodiment of the American dream. He was the only child of a wealthy New York City family. His mother was a young model who caught the attention of every guy in any room she walked into. On the other hand, Frederick's father grew up poor but managed to leverage his connections from college into running a successful venture capital firm in Manhattan. "His words are syrup, his actions are daggers," was the way Frederick described his dad's personality. As a result of his parents' success, Frederick attended a reputable private school downtown. All the old money New York City kids attended school on the Upper East Side. Frederick's family was new money, and he used that to his advantage. Frederick's father never reconciled the fact that his son loved other boys. After coming out, the friction between Frederick's parents was palpable and they ultimately split. Frederick rarely sees his father, but a check for a thousand dollars arrives every year in the mail on his birthday like clockwork. On the other hand, Frederick's mother couldn't seal her disappointment that he didn't move to Connecticut to attend Yale.

"So anyway, what a hunk my Partner Dylan is!" Frederick exclaimed to break up the poignant moment and save them both from embarrassment. Neither of them liked to show emotion and be vulnerable, but sometimes it happens when least expected. Dylan offered up no friction whatsoever. Frederick couldn't deny his unbridled affection for Dylan.

"At least one of us has a good partner! I even declined Patrick's invitation for coffee tomorrow morning," Amelia responded.

"Girl, are you crazy? He's more handsome than any other guy you've ever dated!" Frederick protested.

"No distractions! I mean it!" yelled Amelia. Just then they heard a screechy voice coming from the stairwell.

"You guys know you aren't supposed to be up here," nagged Deborah, the sanctimonious, overzealous, personality-devoid resident assistant.

"We're coming, we're coming," Frederick unenthusiastically murmured, like an elementary school student having to return to class after recess.

Chapter 6: Rehearsals

The next day, rehearsals were set to begin at noon. The prior evening conversation with Frederick prompted Amelia to have a change of heart. Amelia showed up at the infamous coffee shop hoping to find Patrick there and start over on the right foot so they would work well together during the auditions. The aroma that engulfed her as she entered the shop reminded her of waking up during her childhood as her parents brewed their own coffee using espresso beans from Europe. This was probably the reason Amelia kept going back to this coffee shop instead of buying bags of tea from the grocery store and making tea at her apartment. Amelia thought showing up to the coffee shop would break the ice. Patrick was happily surprised to see Amelia as he stood in line to order his Irish coffee.

Patrick jokingly put both hands up in a dramatic fashion. "Don't worry, I did not bring Ballare with me this morning. I wouldn't want you to sue me," Amelia laughed. "Lawyer's promise, I will not sue your cute little puppy," Patrick assured her as he put his right hand up in the air like he was about to testify in a courtroom. "You are a lawyer? No way!" Amelia asked. "There's a lot about me that would surprise you.

Just wait and you will find out, partner," Patrick laughed. "Well, there's some things you need to know about me. I don't drink coffee, only tea. And I am allergic to dairy," Amelia responded, blushing.

"You're no longer in the southwest and since you're my partner, I need you to be at your best. I find that a black Irish Coffee with a dash of cinnamon and a shot of espresso is the perfect precursor to dance rehearsals. No dairy required." Amelia nodded in agreement. "She'll have what I'm having," Patrick said to the barista. The barista paused with a quizzical look on her face and then a big smile was painted on her face like a rainbow that appears after a midday rainstorm in Florida during the summer.

The first day of dance rehearsals went smoothly. Amelia and Patrick got along swimmingly. They learned a simple dance routine that they were to memorize to pass the first round of eliminations. The routine was basic, and Amelia was relieved that Patrick seemed to catch on easily. They made plans to practice in Patrick's studio the next day, as they had the day off and wanted to utilize that extra time to perfect their performance. Amelia arrived at Patrick's apartment with two Irish coffees, both customized to his recommended preferences. It was a thoughtful gesture that did not go unnoticed by Patrick. It reminded him of how un-thoughtful his ex-girlfriend Victoria had been.

After two hours of nonstop practicing, they decided to sit down and take a break. Patrick asked, "So what brought you all the way to New York City?"

Amelia felt compelled to open up to him at that moment. "My parents passed away, and I guess I wanted to get as lost in the big city and simultaneously pursue my parents' dream of becoming a social worker," Amelia replied. "I could ask you the same thing."

Patrick answered, "Fair enough. I also came here to pursue a dream that wasn't possible in Boston and, subconsciously, I think I did it to get out of an unhealthy relationship with my ex-girlfriend. I always knew deep down that she wouldn't follow me here. At the same time, I released myself from an unhealthy relationship with my career."

Chapter 7: Dylan

Amelia met Patrick for an Irish coffee, with almond milk and cinnamon, the next morning before the first found of eliminations were to be announced. Amelia was so nervous early that morning, so much that she clenched her jaw so hard the bonding between two of her teeth came out. Thankfully the bonding was towards the back of her mouth, but there was still a gap, and she did not feel her best self, standing next to her hunky dance partner in the coffee shop that morning.

They hurried down the street to the dance studio, neither of them saying a word. Amelia always stayed silent in times of stress. She referred to herself as an "internalizer" as opposed to an externalizer. Patrick was like Amelia in this way. People on the sidewalk were yelling, cursing, laughing, asking for money, yet Amelia and Patrick were able to drown out all that New York City noise on their way to the studio.

One of the judges, a middle-aged woman with hazel eyes and long chestnut hair, was standing at the front by the front door talking to the cleaning professional who was just heading home from her overnight shift. Amelia noticed the blonde woman had given the cleaner a breakfast sandwich to eat on her way home. *How Kind,* Amelia thought to herself. Patrick noticed Amelia take note of the kind deed. "That's one of the judges, Charisse. My mom used to live in New York and they are old friends. That's how I found out about this opportunity. She doesn't know me though, I have never met her in person, just pictures from years ago. Same hazel eyes." Patrick, whose nerves prevented him from sipping his coffee, walked up to Charisse, and asked, "Would you like an Irish coffee, since you gave your breakfast sandwich away. You'll need the energy today." Charisse responded, "That's sweet, but I only drink green tea and no milk. I appreciate your kind offer."

Amelia and Patrick passed the first round of eliminations with flying colors. Unsurprisingly, Frederick and his partner, Dylan, passed as well. All four of them went out as a group that night to celebrate. It was a motley assortment of people. They finally could take a breath since they had the next two days off from rehearsals. Amelia was eager to officially introduce her dancing partner to her college class partner. Frederick was enamored with his own dancing partner, Dylan, and it showed. They went to a small relatively unknown bar in the east village that sold five-dollar glasses of Scotch and Irish Whiskey. You couldn't find these prices anywhere else in Manhattan, so it became a staple for college students and struggling entertainers. The group first cheered with glasses of Irish Whiskey in honor of Patrick and welcoming him to the city.

As Frederick's best friend, Amelia noticed the subtle stares, the extra forced laughs and body language that he could not hide when interacting with Dylan. Frederick, too, couldn't help but notice Amelia flirting with Patrick in a way that he'd never seen her act with any other guy. She'd deny the flirting later, of course, but it was obvious she was quite taken with him.

Amelia, who had precipitously decreased her alcoholic intake post college, started to feel that rush of calm and energetic feelings both while only can be caused by alcohol. It was the first time in a while that she felt relaxed and very chatty. In contrast, Patrick was from a heavy drinking Irish family and had the tolerance level of a bull. He was delighted to see a lighter side of her than the version of her he met during their first meeting in the coffee shop. Together, they formed a complete yin yang. It was a concept Amelia learned when she started taking hot yoga classes in New York- something she could never do in Arizona. Her favorite class was the Thursday night candlelit Yin classes. Taking part in these classes encouraged her journey to limit her alcohol intake over recent years.

"So, Dylan, tell us more about yourself," Patrick said, always making sure to include everyone and make everyone feel comfortable. Amelia noticed this endearing quality, and it made her feel at ease as well as in awe of Patrick. "Thanks for asking," Dylan replied. Up until that point in the night, Dylan had been very reserved, but the words seemed to flow out of his mouth effortlessly.

Dylan explained that he had all the familial love and support in the world, but no money. Dylan moved to New York to live out his dream of being a dancer and secondarily to be able to support his parents for the rest of their lives. Dylan's mother worked as a housekeeper at the nearby hotel, while his father was a dancer at a tourist-trap live entertainment restaurant in town. His father dragged him to work on days when his mother had to work overnight shifts at the hotel, and Dylan had a sneaking suspicion that's where his love for dancing originated. The others were in awe of Dylan's story. He had a coy way of commanding attention and evoking emotion through his moral sincerity.

Never too shy to interrupt a silent moment, Frederick chimed in to tease Patrick. "You know, Patrick, I wasn't going to say anything, but as someone who grew up with season tickets to the Yankees, I can't really be seen with you in that Red Sox hat. I'm going to have to ask you to lose the hat," Frederick joked. "Never! I was born wearing this hat. It does not come off." Patrick protested. "Well, that reminds me, I should have worn my Marlins hat," Dylan added. "Oh yeah, and I should have worn my Phoenix Suns hate," Amelia said, trying to sound like she knew what she was talking about. "Good try, but wrong sport!" Frederick blurted out. They all shared a laugh.

There they sat, four people from different regions of the country, and different walks of life, laughing together in a small New York City bar. Amelia laughed so hard, her abdomen muscles felt like she'd been doing crunches all day and her smile widened as much as it used to when she spent time with her family. Frederick, unable to control his own laughter or catch his breath, pointed at her face. "Whoa, what happened there!" Dylan shouted, joining in on the silliness. Amelia was as confused as ever but continued to laugh with them. Patrick shouted, "You're missing a tooth you hillbilly!" as he grabbed his own abdomen muscles and bent over in laughter. That's when Amelia realized they had all noticed the gap in her mouth caused by her nerves this morning. Amelia instantaneously snapped out of it and mortification enveloped her. Blotches of redness rapidly started appearing on her neck and cheeks as usual anytime she felt embarrassed.

Amelia did what she did best when feeling vulnerable; she lashed out, caused a fight, and ran away. "I'm not missing a tooth. Just some bonding, you fool!" Frederick followed Amelia out the door. "Please don't be mad at Patrick. I'm the one who pointed it out. I thought we were having fun," Frederick said as he pleaded with her to stay. "I'm out of here!" Amelia shouted. The very next morning, Amelia made an emergency visit with her dentist and filled the gap between her teeth, but no dental procedure could heal the hole in her heart.

Chapter 8: Times Square

Patrick spent his first morning off thinking of ways to get back in Amelia's good graces. His time in the big city had been such a whirlwind thus far, so this day was the first time he was left to his own devices. He couldn't bring himself to get out of bed, leave the tiny apartment, and start his day. As he lay in bed, Patrick started to think about Veronica and romanticize their time in Boston. He thought about how different it would be if she had been here with him. On the other hand, he was grateful that she wasn't there to criticize him and make him feel worse about himself. She also wouldn't be too fond of Patrick being paired up with a gorgeous dancing partner.

Amelia was sweet, kind, and a stark contrast to Veronica. But somehow Patrick had hurt her feelings, and he couldn't stop beating himself up about it. He should be celebrating the minor victory of making it past the first round of auditions. Nothing he ever did seemed to be good enough for any woman he ever dated or liked. Patrick still wasn't sure how much he liked Amelia, but one thing was sure, he loved her laugh. Just then, a light bulb turned on in his head. *That's how I'll make it up to her,* Patrick thought to himself, *I have to make her laugh.*

The goal of finding a way to make Amelia laugh was motivation enough to get Patrick out of bed and on the move. As a licensed attorney, Patrick was anything, it was goal oriented. Once he had a goal in mind, you can bet your money he was going to meet that goal. The first thing Patrick did was start walking down the streets of Times Square for some humor inspiration.

Patrick walked past the newly renovated toy store in the center of Times Square. It reminded him of his favorite Christmas movie, Home Alone 2. The newest Disney Pixar movie apparently starred a green, animal-like creature with a missing tooth. Before he could amend himself, Patrick bumped into a person dressed up as a fuzzy green character, the same character on the posters for the new Disney Pixar movie that Patrick never heard of. The physical contact must've knocked some sense into Patrick's brain because he instantly had an epiphany. Patrick decided that he would make light of the whole "toothless hillbilly" situation and hope that Amelia would understand the joke. It was the only idea he had at that moment, so Patrick gathered the courage to follow through on his devious plan of making Amelia smile, and he waltzed himself into the toy store. As he suspected, green, toothless stuffed animals lined the walls in front of the store. There was even a little dog costume to match the stuffed animals. Perfect. Patrick had almost forgotten about Ballare. If he wanted to get back in Amelia's good graces, he'd have to find a way to charm Ballare. Patrick purchased the stuffed animal and dog costume, and he was ready to carry out his plan for better or for worse. He was hopeful that things would turn out in his favor. As Patrick walked out of the toy store, a random gust of wind blew off his Red Sox hat off of his head and it disappeared into the sky before he had the chance to grab it. He made eye contact with the person dressed up as the green animal, who just shrugged his shoulders and Patrick imagined there was a look of pity on his face underneath his mask.

It was a long walk back to the East Village from Times Square without his hat. This had never happened in Boston, even on those windy winter days in the harbor, nor on those windy days sailing on the Charles River. Patrick couldn't replace the hat because it had significant sentimental value. Patrick's grandfather had bought him the hat when he was too young to remember and told him the hat should remind him to always follow his dreams. At the time, Patrick wanted to be a baseball player for the Boston Red Sox, starting pitcher to be exact, but his dreams changed since graduating elementary school. *There's no point in crying over spilt milk,* Patrick whispered to himself. It was a turn of phrase his mother always said to him growing up.

Patrick continued walking the New York City streets, trying to forget the insurmountable loss of his most beloved hat. He remembered that Frederick mentioned the apartment complex Amelia had lived in right next to their college. Frederick mentioned that he used to meet Amelia there and they walked to class together.

The apartment complex in which Amelia resided wasn't too far from Mocha Lattes Coffee Shop. It was a two-bedroom condo unit on the third floor of a walk up, too fancy for the average college student to afford. Patrick wasn't sure how she afforded such a sumptuous place, but Amelia didn't seem ready to open up about her family beyond their initial conversation, and he certainly didn't want to push her away.

Patrick shook off all his nerves and ran his fingers through his fair, inadvertently reminding himself that he no longer possessed his lucky hat, and as a result, nerves fired through his body like sparklers on the Fourth of July. Patrick stood there in the foyer of Amelia's building and pressed every apartment buzzer on the third floor until he heard her dulcet-toned voice. Ballare's guttural growl was low, yet constant in the background as Amelia dubiously agreed to let Patrick up. "I couldn't find an olive branch, but consider this a peace offering," Patrick said as he presented Amelia and Ballare with the toothless stuffed animal and dog costume. Amelia had an incredulous look on her face before bursting into laughter. Ballare hopped up like a bunny and grabbed the dog costume with her teeth. Although not gifted for its intended use, Patrick was happy to see Ballare enjoy his gift, even if that meant watching it being ripped to pieces. Amelia was laughing on the floor and Ballare was pleasantly entertained. *My diabolical plan worked out after all;* Patrick maniacally laughed at himself.

Patrick walked back to his temporary New York City home. From a block away, Patrick spotted something red gleaming from the bike rack in front of his apartment like a broken, flashing traffic signal. As he approached the bike rack, it became clearer that there was a Red Sox logo on the hat. Patrick was in disbelief. The odds of it being the same hat that flew off his head as he was leaving earlier in the day were very low.

The only way of verifying the authenticity of the hat was to inspect it for chew marks on the side. The origin of the chew marks was from his parents' golden retriever, Brody, stealing his hat years ago and chewing it up before Patrick had the chance to get it back. Patrick found the chew marks endearing and thought it gave the hat character and made it nuanced. It also was a bittersweet reminder of Brody after he passed away. Brody was the beloved family dog, and Patrick had a special bond with him that could never be replaced. Therefore, Patrick never even considered getting a dog of his own, as it would be an inferior replacement. Patrick stopped and thought about Brody for a moment, and then his attention turned back to the hat.

Patrick picked up the hat and inspected it. It was in fact his original Boston Red Sox baseball cap, dog chew marks and all. This hat was the embodiment of hope for Patrick, and he vowed never to lose it again.

Chapter 9: Professor Bryant

Frederick walked to Amelia's apartment to have breakfast with her before their morning psychology class. Since they had the day off from auditions, they didn't have to skip class again, but they did expect to feel Professor Bryant's wrath from missing all last week. He didn't necessarily take attendance for the entire class of two hundred people, but their presence was always known, and their absence always felt. Nothing got past Professor Bryant.

"I can't afford to fail this class and have my parents think I'm a failure," Frederick lamented. "Well, I don't have parents, but I still can't fail. I need a backup plan if I don't get through these auditions. Professor Bryant despises us, and we missed the past two weeks of classes," Amelia responded. "I know! I know! Let's stop at Mocha Lattes on the way to class and pick up a tasty blueberry Fritter for him. I hear his wife used to bring him one each morning before she passed away," Frederick suggested. "The thought of one of those blueberry fritters is making my stomach suddenly desperate for sweets. Thanks for tempting me with sweets while I'm supposed to be in tip top shape!" Amelia argued. "So, Mocha Lattes it is?" Frederick asked. "I have a feeling you're not going to take no for an answer, and I don't have the wherewithal to come up with a defense. Fine," Amelia responded, feeling defeated.

Mocha Lattes had finally commenced their Christmas decoration set up. Amelia cherished the Christmas spirit and decorating in New York City. One of the baristas was wobbling on a latter attempting to hang up white strands of light on the front of the store. Another barista was trying to find a place to plug in the reindeer out front so it would light up. "It's official, Christmas is here," Frederick vibrantly shouted. Although Frederick grew up in New York City, he never became cynical or unappreciative of the magic of Christmas that could only be felt in the big city. The love of Christmas was something that Amelia and Frederick had in common.

Frederick ordered, "I'll take the Holly Donut Holes, two blueberry fritters, one Christmas Caramel Latte and one green tea with almond milk, both extra-large." He had Amelia's order memorized down to a cup of tea. "Actually, I think I will order an Irish coffee, no tea. And why two blueberry fritters?" Amelia inquired. "Yes, there's no better time to treat yourself than Christmas. You deserve it," Frederick insisted as the barista handed the blueberry fritters to Amelia. "I can't argue with that," Amelia stated as she ripped open the wax paper and took a big bite out of the blueberry fritter. It tasted like a mixture of happiness, Christmas spirit and a burst of energy.

Amelia closed her eyes for a few seconds to take in the indulgent moment, while Frederick was adding ice cubes to his latte to cool it off. Why not just order an iced latte she always wondered, but Frederick was a nuanced person and so she never bothered to ask. Amelia's eyes blinked open the second she heard a familiar voice. "I see you've taken my advice," Patrick said, pointing at the Irish coffee. Amelia turned around and accidentally knocked her coffee into Patrick's elbow, and it spilled over the floor on splattered onto the decorative Christmas garland. "I see we've come full circle," Patrick tried to laugh off the incident while inside he was processing the pain of the hot coffee burning through his elbow and arm. Amelia sighed in embarrassment. "Let's call it even," she declared.

Frederick had added four cubes of ice in his latte before realizing the incident that had just occurred. Thanks to his parents' divorce, Frederick was adept at drowning out the chaos when focusing on accomplishing a task, such as cooling off a latte. "Oh man, we are going most certainly going to be late for Professor Bryant's class," Frederick murmured softly. "Hello Patrick, fancy to see you here. Have you tried the blueberry fritters?" Frederick asked, trying to change the subject and minimize Amelia's embarrassment. "Late to class, got to go," Amelia interrupted as she grabbed Frederick's arm and pulled him out the door.

As they walked to class, Frederick couldn't help but ask, "So, what was that all about? Are you and Patrick still at odds? By the way, my arm is sore, and you owe me a massage!" "I may have omitted this information, but Patrick came over the other day and presented an olive branch that I couldn't refuse. He was very sweet. All is forgiven," Amelia stated. "Oh really? You just forgot to mention this? You never act this coy with a guy. I think you really like him. Admit it or face your peril!" Frederick demanded. "Fine, since you're my best friend, I will disclose that I sort of like him. Hopefully spilling coffee all over him did not tarnish his view of me. Also, all my energy needs to be focused on the dance auditions," Amelia replied.

Amelia followed Frederick into the classroom as they tried to brush off the fact that they were twenty minutes late. Luckily, the class broke into smaller groups having side conversations and Professor

Bryant was distracted on a phone call. As Professor Bryant ended the phone call and looked up from his desk, Frederick presented the box with the blueberry fritter inside.

Professor Bryant rolled his eyes as he asked, "And what may I ask is inside this mysterious box?" "Something so delicious it'll make you forget all about our absences and tardiness," Frederick replied, with his quick wit. Professor Bryant opened the box and inspected the blueberry fritter with a wistful look in his eyes. "This was incredibly thoughtful and kind. Blueberry is my absolute favorite," he stated right before he bit into the fritter. After finishing his first bite, Professor Bryant continued, "However sweet this gesture may be, and I won't ask how you knew my favorite flavored fritter, but this will not excuse your absences without an explanation." Amelia pleaded, "Please, we will do anything to make it up to you. We have been attending dance rehearsals and going through audition rounds to be chosen for the opportunity of a lifetime. If we pass the auditions, we will land a spot in the Times Square New Year's Eve Dance Special, which is televised nationally. We'll do extra credit, anything to make it up to you while not letting this other dream of ours slip away."

Professor Bryant sat quietly for a moment with a pensive look on his face and his hand resting under his chin. "I have a proposition for both of you. I wouldn't want this course to get in the way of your dreams, and I understand the financial burden of being a college student as I once was one myself, believe it or not. Physical exercise, teamwork, and competition are all parts of psychology. I'll allow you to miss class periodically for rehearsals. If you both end up passing the final audition and dancing in the show, I'll waive the final and your final grade will be an A. On the other hand, if even one of you does not pass the final audition, you will both take the final and your final grade will be solely dependent on that score. Agreed?" Frederick had a quizzical look on his face as Amelia looked incredulously at Professional Bryant. "Is this a trick?" Frederick asked. "What he meant to say is yes, agreed, on behalf of both of us," Amelia interrupted. The quizzical look on Frederick's face was still frozen in disbelief. Professor Bryant reached out to initiate a handshake with each of them. "One more thing, if either of you pass the final audition, I want a front row ticket to the show," Professor Bryant added. "Done!" Amelia and Frederick shouted in unison like robots.

After class, Amelia and Frederick walked back home. "Crisis Averted!" Amelia exclaimed. "I'm still in shock. Didn't know Professor Bryant had it in him," Frederick added. "It was the blueberry fritter, and the memory of his late wife. "You're a genius, Frederick," Amelia replied. "Oh stop, you're making me blush. The blueberry fritter was genius though if I don't say so myself. Very New England," Frederick laughed.

Chapter 10: Kelly

Charisse left Mocha Lattes, struggling to balance a carton of coffee in her left hand and a bag with breakfast sandwich stowed away under her armpit. In her right hand, she had a cup of green tea with almond milk for herself. She wanted to surprise her fellow judges with a morning pick me up as auditions were set to resume. The breakfast sandwich was for the overnight cleaning professional who was always so polite and friendly to Charisse in the mornings as she left at the end of her shift. Charise loved to see the spark in people's eyes when she caught them off guard by doing something thoughtful and kind, even the smallest of gestures could light up someone's eyes and make their day. Charisse was now a judge for the Times Square New Year's Eve Dance Special. She was chosen after an impressive career as a dancer and choreographer in New York City for several years.

As her phone buzzed, Charisse nearly stumbled to the ground but impressively maintained her balance and answered the call with her phone tucked between her neck and ear. "Kelly, is that you?" Charisse asked the familiar voice on the other end of the phone call. It was impossible to forget her dear friend's voice. "It's your old roomie!

Surprise! I'm in town, Charry!" Kelly yelled into the phone in her high pitch Irish accent." Charisse stopped in her tracks. She hadn't seen Kelly in years. Kelly was one of her first friends in New York City and they were roommates before Kelly fell in love and moved to Boston to start a family. Kelly was one of those people who were long winded, but the end result was worth the wait. "Oh my! No one has called me Charry in years! I'm about to spill four coffees and a tea all over me. I'm judging auditions this morning, but let's get together this evening. So excited! Text me the address where you're staying, roomie!" Charisse responded, attempting to contain her excitement while still juggling her purchases from Mocha Lattes. "You got it roomie! I'll text you later," Kellie replied and then ended the phone call.

After what seemed like the long walk of her life, Charisse made it to the dance studio. Unfortunately, she was too late to catch the cleaning professional leaving the studio, so she gave the breakfast sandwich to a homeless person who was sitting right outside on the corner of the block. Charisse presented the four coffees to the other judges, although they were no longer hot, and she sipped her lukewarm green tea. Still, they each graciously thanked her. "Now, time to get these auditions started," Charisse announced.

The first half of the day, the dancers were taught a moderately difficult partner routine that would be performed in pairs. The rest of the day would be spent practicing while the judges noted how well the pairs of dancers practiced together. The judges were homing in on how well each pair of dancers worked together. Charisse had spent weeks choreographing this dance routine. Teamwork and charisma were the most important factors judges took into consideration when selecting dancers for shows. Charisse saw something in a young pair of dancers working together in the back of the room. Charisse pointed this observation out to her fellow judges. "Look at that teamwork in the back corner. I can see them working together and can feel chemistry. Let's keep an eye on that pair," she whispered to the other judge sitting next to her. The other judge looked up and started observing the pair. The young female dancer had chestnut hair tightly pulled back and neatly twisted into a bun sitting on top of her head. The male dancer, with blonde hair, fair skin, and freckles, complimented her perfectly. Nearly a foot taller than the female, he was able to effortlessly lift the female by the waist as she gracefully nailed a split in the air and landed in his arms. The pair turned around after the beautiful display and Charisse recognized the freckles and blue eyes. The male dancer was none other than the son of her old best friend. Charisse knew she would have to have a discussion with the other judges about recusing herself from the rest of their auditions.

Charisse took one of the judges, Judy, aside after the dancers were done for the day and went home. Charisse explained that one of her best friends' sons was auditioning for the show and that she hadn't recognized him nor known his name until that very day. Charisse further noted that she would likely be meeting him since his mother, her good friend, was in town. Judy informed Charisse that she must promise not to speak of the auditions with him and then Judy reassured Charisse that she would meet with the other judges to relay the information to them. "I don't foresee the other judges having an issue with this," Judy stated. "Thank you so much, Judy. I don't want anything to get in the way of this kid's opportunity," Charisse responded. "Now go on and see your old friend. Take a break from worrying too much!" Judy demanded. Charisse once again thanked Judy and then exited the studio for the day.

Charisse immediately picked up her phone as she stepped outside. She had been waiting all day to get in touch with her dear friend Kelly. "Roomie!" Kelly cheered on the other end of the phone so loudly that Charisse had to pull it off her ear and the woman walking fifty feet behind her could hear the greeting. "Hold on one second, I have an important call on the other line," Charisse said. Charisse quickly swapped the call and put the phone back up to her ear. The woman walking behind her became increasingly frustrated and eventually passed Charisse as she was fumbling with her phone. "It's me, Judy. The other judges are fine with the arrangement. Moving forward, you will recuse yourself from Patrick's auditions. Other than that, we are excited about the direction of the show. See you soon!" Charisse let out a sigh of relief as she responded, "You're the best, Judy." Charisse called Kelly back and finalized dinner plans at Riverpark restaurant in East Village.

Chapter 11: Quiet Place

Patrick was blindsided by a call from his mother, Kelly, on his walk home from the dance studio following a grueling day of auditions. In most circumstances, he would not take a phone call while Amelia was standing right next to him, but his mother never just called out of the blue for no reason. Clearly, she was up to something, and it wasn't good.

"Patrick, come to Marriot Marquis Times Square at once!" Kelly yelled into the phone. "Mom, what are you talking about? I am in East Village. Not to mention, you nearly blew off my ear just now," Patrick responded, feeling frustrated at her evasiveness. "Well honey, can you just turn around and walk to Times Square or better yet, take a cab?" Kelly asked. "And is that where you are mother dearest?" Patrick asked sarcastically, already knowing the answer. "You know me too well son. Yes, I made the executive decision to come visit my favorite kid and my best friend. There's a rotating restaurant at the top of my hotel and I want to treat you. Bring your dancer friends if you want!" Kelly offered. "You made a reservation before even telling me you're in the city?" Patrick responded, not at all surprised by his mom's behavior. "I'm an eternal optimist. What can I say? Reservation for four at 7:00pm just in case you decide to bring along a dancer friend." Kelly responded. She was never one to miss a beat.

Patrick ended the call, and his cheeks turned red as he realized Amelia had been closely monitoring his call with his mother and a smirk appeared across her face.

Because he had no other option, Patrick smiled and shrugged. "Mothers. Can't live with them, can't live…" Amelia solemnly finished his sentence, "without them." Patrick realized that he was saying this to someone who had no choice but to live without her mother. He immediately regretted saying something so insensitive just because he was embarrassed that Amelia overheard his phone conversation without his own mother. *Sometimes insecurity is worse than the thing you're insecure about,* Patrick told himself. "Amelia, I am so incredibly sorry. I didn't think about what I was saying. Please forgive me." "No need to apologize. I have fond memories of my mother, and I feel like she's still with me. I'm fine," Amelia responded.

Patrick wasn't convinced that Amelia was fine at that very moment, and he was desperate to change the subject. "I have an idea.

How about you meet my mother? At the very least, you'll get a lovely meal," Patrick insisted. "I can't meet anyone new right now. May hair is a puffy mess with this rain and humidity today—Amelia stopped herself-- You know what. I would love to," Amelia gave in. "Well, you heard my mother, reservation at 7. I'll show you the way," Patrick offered. "I think I know my way to the Marriot Marquis rotating restaurant! I've spent many brunch dates there," Amelia responded. They both laughed in unison.

Amelia and Patrick made their way to the hotel. "I love going up the glass elevators and viewing the entire hotel bar and lobby. It's the ultimate people watching experience!" Amelia exclaimed. "On the contrary, those glass elevators make me feel that everyone is people watching me." Patrick disagreed. "Sometimes I feel like you're the yin to my yang," Amelia admitted. Patrick felt a shock go through his body in response to the warm comment. Amelia blushed and red blotches appeared on her chest as she processed the words that came out of her mouth and what they meant. Neither of them was susceptible to allowing their inner thoughts and feelings to be released into the world.

Amelia and Patrick made their way up the glass elevators onto the fiftieth floor. Patrick was sweating through his shirt during the entire elevator ride up. The only other girl that he ever introduced to his mother was Veronica, and that ended in disaster. Kelly never warmed up to Veronica and any family gathering was a source of contention. Veronica led him down a primrose path of debauchery. These worries raced through Patrick's mind faster with every floor the elevator passed. The elevator was silent, as if it was full of strangers trying to mind their own business. Finally, the elevator reached floor fifty and that high pitched bell rang. *Just another audition to pass, no big deal,* Patrick whispered to himself, although his body disagreed with his words. The back of his throat was burning.

The room was filled with a thick silence except for the sound of forks scraping against plates. And then a shouting woman abruptly ended the silence. "My son, my son!" Kelly chanted so enthusiastically that every restaurant patron turned around as if a famous person had just arrived. Both Patrick and Amelia simultaneously turned red like they had just returned from a long day at the beach. Despite auditioning for a nationally televised show, neither Patrick nor Amelia preferred to be in the spotlight when the dancing component was removed from the equation. Amelia followed Patrick to meet his mother, almost becoming roadkill as a waitress power walked towards her with a plate of sizzling chicken saltimbocca.

"Yes, mother dearest, it is in fact your son. Must you make it known to the entire restaurant?" Patrick asked. "Oh, give me a kiss, kiddo!" Kelly demanded. She wrapped her hands around Patrick and made eye contact with Amelia. "You must be Patrick's dancing partner! So glad you came!" Kelly excitedly exclaimed. Patrick smiled as Kelly wrapped her arms around Amelia and gave her a warm hug and then took a breath in. The smell of garlic and onion assaulted them—it was Italian night.

Patrick spotted a familiar face on the other side of this mother's hug—it was the generous judge, Charisse. Charisse directed her attention to Amelia and Patrick. "It is an absolute pleasure to formally meet you both and let me lead by stating you are both incredibly talented," Charisse stated. Patrick observed Amelia's eyes light up. "The pleasure is all mine. I've been a fan of your choreography work for years. You have inspired me to enter this competition. And I'm not just saying that because you're a judge!" Amelia joked as an attempt to break the ice. "Oh no, I have already recused myself from your auditions. No competition talks at this dinner!" Charisse laughed. "Fine by me," Patrick added.

The foursome sat at a window table that Kelly had specially reserved. At one time, a window seat was the ultimate view of Manhattan, but eventually taller buildings sprouted up nearly twice as tall. The waitress handed out plates with fruit and vegetable patterns decorating the borders. She placed a mouthwatering basket of garlic knots dripping in olive oil and butter. Patrick took one and slowly licked it like a piece of candy. "This garlic knot has transported me back in time to North End in Boston. Yum!" said Patrick. "Amelia, did you know that Boston North End has the best Italian food in the country?" Kelly asked. "I did not, but as someone who grew up in Arizona, I am not that well versed in fine Italian cuisine," Amelia responded as she grabbed a garlic knot. She brushed Patrick's hand as he was grabbing for his second helping and they exchanged sweeping glances. After the first bite, Amelia immediately felt the calories entering her blood stream.

"No Way! You hail from the Grand Canyon State?" Charisse asked Amelia. Amelia responded, "I am! I grew up in the golf capital of the United States- Scottsdale. Why do you ask?" Amelia responded to Charisse's question with a question of her own. "I am also from the West's most Western Town," Charisse laughed. "That's what my mom used to call it!" Amelia responded. "I'm feeling consigned to oblivion. I don't know southwest small talk," Kelly added. "Oh yes, us "Yankeeland" people don't understand Arizona talk," Patrick joked. "Sorry! It's unwonted to bump into another Arizonian on the east coast," Charisse apologized. "That's for certain," Amelia said.

The waitress walked over to their table and apologized for the delay, simultaneously offering to take their food and drink order. Kelly was first to order: "I'll have an Irish car bomb, water, and Caesar salad. Patrick was next: "I'll order an Irish car bomb, club soda and chicken saltimbocca. Amelia was next to order: "For my drink I will have green tea with almond milk and for my meal I will have eggplant parmesan, hold the parmesan." Patrick and Kelly made eye contact and shared a befuddled look. "I also am allergic to dairy," Charisse interjected, "I will have a green tea with almond milk also, and the whole wheat pasta primavera with olives added." Patrick and Kelly looked at Amelia and Charisse as if they were extraneous creatures walking among them. "May I also order a side of plain pasta to go for my dog? I didn't get to stop home and feed her dinner this evening," Amelia inquired. The waitress assured her it wouldn't be a problem.

"Thanks for understanding. I've always had an unexplained allergy to milk," Amelia unnecessarily apologized. "Well, that's two offbeat things we have in common," Charisse declared. "So, how do you and Kelly know each other?" Amelia asked. "We were roommates back in the day when I first came to New York City. Conjointly, she was my first and dearest friend," Charisse responded. Kelly smiled, "I couldn't have said it better myself. New York City was very intimidating compared to Boston. Still is, wouldn't you say so yourself Patrick?" Patrick answered, "Agreed. Manhattan alone has more people than the entire city limits of Boston. It's easy to get lost in the crowd here." "Although right now it feels like a small world, wouldn't you agree Charisse and Amelia?" Kelly asked. Both ladies expressed agreement in unison.

Just as the conversation was flowing readily, the waitress brought over the sumptuous looking food with the help of the bus boy. The silence that followed was the result of a combination of the group's collective hunger and the heavenly tasting food. Fast forward fifteen minutes, each of them was scraping their plates clean. The only sounds were knives granulating against the old school Italian, flower-decorated plates. Kelly excused herself to use the restroom.

On the way to the restroom, she surreptitiously made a beeline for the hostess stand to ask for the check. Kelly called this act the "Irish Treat." The "Irish Treat" consisted of quietly leaving the dinner table to find the hostess and provide payment for the entire table so the tab is already paid and no one else can chip in. In Patrick and Kelly's family, it became a competition to see who can pay first at every restaurant, which is why they eventually decided to gather for most family meals at home in Kelly's kitchen. Kelly's kitchen was Patrick's happy place.

Kelly returned to the table with a suspicious smirk on her face. Patrick promptly knew that Kelly had just completed the "Irish Treat" and he laughed inside knowing that Charisse and Amelia were completely in the dark as to what Kelly just pulled off. "What are you two up to? Is there some kind of mother-son facial expression communication that I'm not aware of?" Charisse sarcastically asked. "Don't look at me!" Patrick responded as he turned and winked at his mother. Kelly grinned and held up the receipt. "You always beat me to the punch!" Charisse complained. Amelia chimed in, "Now I feel like I am the only one out of the loop!" Charisse clued Amelia in, "Kelly does this thing where she sneaks away to the 'bathroom' but pays the tab. She can't help herself. Her generosity is out of control." Amelia laughed. Introspectively, Amelia was thinking how unexpectedly delightful it had been to be around these people, like winter snow coming down on the beach in Maine.

The group left the restaurant after coming to the realization that Kelly was not going to allow anyone else to pay for their meal. They walked down the block and past a bar called, "Terry's Karaoke Klub." Unfailingly, Kelly couldn't resist the temptation to have while simultaneously embarrassing her son. Kelly got the attention of the group and pointed to the bar.

Patrick instantly sensed what Kelly was thinking. "Mom, just no!" Patrick protested. But he already knew that his mother always gets what she wants once she has an idea in her head and puts her mind to it. Patrick could hear the advice his dad gave him years ago: "When it comes to your mother, it's wiser to ride the wave than to resist."

"Patrick used to love karaoke when he was a young child," Kelly revealed to Charisse and Amelia. "Aww," they both responded in unison. Patrick blushed and his eye started twitching. He became cognizant of the fact that he was being outnumbered by women "awing" at him, and he managed to sidestep the whole singing thing. Dancing was much more his forte.

"I must use the restroom before we go," said Kelly, awkwardly and nervously trying to break up the tension and allow some space for Patrick and Amelia to process the last few minutes. "Oh, right, I as well," Charisse said as she followed Kelly to the bathroom.

Amelia lumberingly walked over to Patick. "Amelia, it's been such a pleasure getting to know you, personally and professionally. I think I'm really starting to—" Patrick said before Amelia interrupted, "Me too. I was a little apprehensive at first but you're very special." Patrick softened his gaze and felt his eyelids get heavy. Amelia closed her eyes and let herself inch closer to him. Unanticipatedly, before they had a chance to kiss, Amelia heard a recognizable voice. Patrick and Amelia opened their eyes, backed away from each other, and turned their heads towards the voice, in unison like an Olympic synchronized swimmer routine.

"Amelia, fancy to find you guys here in a karaoke bar on a school night!" shouted Professor Bryant. *Of all the places in New York City to run into a professor, it had to be here, in a karaoke bar, after professing my adornment to a man for the first time*, Amelia thought to herself.

It was a common case of bad timing. And seeing Professor Bryant at a karaoke bar was as strange as seeing a puppy in a zoo. He seemed different than he did in the classroom: more confident, less nerdy. To complicate the moment further, Kelly and Charisse walked over and joined the group. Professor Bryant and Charisse immediately locked their eyes. Professor Bryant put his hand out to greet Charisse, and he quickly transformed back into the nerdy, awkward professor that she knew him to be. Charisse appeared a little unsteady herself as evidenced by her hand shaking ever so slightly when she accepted

Professor Bryant's greeting. "You may call me Aiden," he said to Charisse. Charisse had a skittish grin stained across her face. Amelia had an incredulous face as she failed to consider whether her professor had a first name or had a life and did things other than be her professor. Kelly curiously took it all in via osmosis.

"Professor Bryant, this is my dancing partner, his mother, and one of our judges," Amelia interjected. Kelly and Patrick politely smiled as they introduced their names. "Oh, so that dancing competition you mentioned is substantial, not just a subterfuge to get out of class," Professor Bryant joked. "How generous and accommodating of you. I can assure you; Amelia is a talented young lady full of potential and lightning doesn't strike twice," Charisse responded. Aiden blushed. "I think it's important for my students to explore all avenues of creativity to make them well rounded," he stated.

"Well, Professor Bryant, we are in a karaoke bar in the wee hours of the morning, so enough of the weighty conversation," Aiden's friend, Theodore, continued, "Please excuse my friend. He doesn't get out much. I had to strong arm him to get here and celebrate my 50th birthday."

"Happy Birthday, Theordore! It's getting late, but since my friend Charisse has off tomorrow, I plan on kidnapping her and forcing her to accompany me to Starbucks New York Roastery in West Village tomorrow morning if your friend, Professor Bryant, feels so inclined to join us. It's a crime to drink Starbucks in New England—I must save face by going to "Dunkies", but I do miss my Starbucks," said Kelly. "That sounds lovely. I might be able to come before class, if I can peel myself out of bed in a timely manner, after this late night," Aiden responded. Aiden and Theordore waved as they walked out of the bar. Kelly and Charisse said their goodbyes and hailed a cab. "Cabs: this is where New York has Boston beat," Kelly stated as they left. And then there were two.

"Please allow me to walk you home," Patrick requested. Amelia was powerless to resist the offer. They walked down the markedly quiet New York streets. "What's your quiet place?" Patrick asked Amelia. "What do you mean?" Amelia replied. "New York is so raucous; you must have a spot where you go to withdraw when you are overwhelmed, you know, when things get too loud. I even had one in Boston," Patrick answered. "You tell me yours first," Amelia said. "There's this little, fairly unknown beach, near Castle Island. I would go in the early afternoon when I needed to think, and then watch the boats go by. I used to take my dog, Brody, when he was still around, since there was a gated dog park nearby," Patrick responded. "That sounds exquisite," Amelia commented. "My quiet place is sitting on the dock by the water overlooking the Statue of Liberty with my dog, Ballare. I take joy in watching the ferry go to and from the statue," Amelia said.

"Let's go there," the words slipped from Patrick's tongue like he was going down a children's slide. "It's a bit of a detour from my apartment, but I'm down," Amelia responded. Patrick followed as Amelia led him past her apartment and to the quiet, dark dock. Only the sound of gentle waves splashing against the dock was audible. Patrick and Amelia sat there soundlessly, bereft of words. Five minutes of silence later, Patrick gathered the courage to put his hand on Amelia's cheek and kiss her. Amelia reciprocated, as she had been waiting for the moment all night. Patrick enveloped Amelia in his arms and they shared the sweetest embrace, right there in Amelia's quiet place. Emotion gathered in the back of her throat, and she lost all self-control.

Chapter 12: Old Friends

Always one to deliver on her promises, Kelly was at the concierge desk of Charisse's building bright and early. As promised at the karaoke bar, she woke up in a timely manner to force Charisse out of bed. In their early days of New York City living, they didn't have enough money to have doormen nor concierge staff, and it was a lot easier for Kelly to show up unannounced at her friends' apartments. The ritual that Kelly missed dearly was going to the Starbucks New York Roastery with Charisse after a long night when they were too exhausted to make their own coffee in their cheap coffee maker. It was their version of gluttony that they could afford in their 20s. This special Starbucks location created a sense of nostalgia within Kelly.

"Please tell Charisse her oldest New York friend is here to carry her out of bed," Kelly joked with the concierge staff. "Sure thing, Ma'am," the concierge responded politely. The concierge dialed Charisse's room and minutes later she was heading up the elevator to the 20th floor and into Charisse's unlocked apartment door without knocking. "What a gorgeous view, can I move in part time?" Kelly asked, half serious. "Not if you wake me up at the crack of dawn on my days off!" Charisse protested. The two of them were bickering like sisters, just like old times.

At Kelly's behest, the best friend duo made it to Starbucks New York Roastery for coffee and breakfast, but not without the help of a cab. "Ah, the espresso beans hit differently in New York," Kelly declared. "I'm going to need a quadruple espresso to wake me up after our long night," Charisse said. "Don't be a Debby Downer, maybe if you had a man in your life, then you wouldn't always go to bed so early!" Kelly said with the type of brutal honesty only a sister could get away with. Right on cue, Aiden walked in. Kelly and Charisse waved him over in unison. "What a surprise, rarely do I get taken up on the token invites," Kelly whispered.

"Top of the morning to you ladies!" Aiden greeted Charisse and Kelly with an upspeak tone. "I figured I'd take you up on that token offer. I don't get very many," Aiden said as he winked at Kelly, almost as if he just ready her mind. Kelly looked puzzled and uncharacteristically at a loss for words. *Well, this is off to an awkward start,* Charisse thought to herself.

"Glad you could make it. I know I barely did," Charisse chimed in. "That's what cabs are for," Aiden laughed. He was clever and charming this morning. Aiden was spreading his wings like a peacock, a transformation that appeared to occur overnight. And Charisse was champing at the bit to peel back all his other layers like an onion.

When Kelly was finally able to gather her thoughts, she said, "So Aiden, tell us more about yourself. What brings you to New York?" "Well, I don't have the most fascinating story," Aiden admitted. "I'm from the outskirts of the city, Westchester to be exact, and went to school and worked here. I got married at an early age but never had any kids. I worked in the social work field for a while and then decided to move into the city and teach after my wife passed away. I'm not good at this, talking about myself. I'm used to talking to students all day long. Sorry, was that too much information? Am I boring you?" Aiden asked apologetically. *How nice to see his vulnerable side,* Charisse thought to herself. "This isn't a job interview, but if it was, I'd give you a second interview," Kelly joked.

"Kelly and I were roommates in the city years ago and I've been here ever since. I bet we've crossed paths at some point," Charisse said.

"Statistically speaking, there is a 15.528% chance of crossing paths with someone you know, but it's unclear what the percentage chance of meeting someone you might know in the future is," Aiden responded, unleashing his inner nerd yet again. Charisse found the nerdiness to be endearing.

"Well, ladies, thanks for the coffee recommendation, but I have some preparation to do for my next lecture. Where shall I bump into you next? Aiden asked sarcastically. He continued, "As General Douglas A. Macarthur once said during World War II in the Philippines 'I shall return.'" Kelly gave Charisse a proverbial nudge with the look of an eye and they both knew what it meant. "Should you need any more coffee recommendations, you can reach me at this number," Charisse said as she handed him a napkin with her number that Kelly had prewritten on it for her. *That was cringeworthy,* she thought to herself. Aiden accepted the napkin and bottled his excitement as he left through the revolving door.

"Good girl!" Kelly joked. "And then there was two. So, what have you planned for the rest of the day?" Charisse asked. "I've always wanted to go on a carriage ride around Central Park," Kelly said. "Oh no, I consider that animal cruelty and I won't allow a horse to carry us around in an oversized carriage," Charisse responded. "But we went dog sledding on our winter trip to Maine," Kelly replied. "Those were rescue dogs from a farm, and we were on a small sled, and they enjoyed doing it," Charisse explained. "Fair enough. How about we take a tour boat ride to the statue of liberty," Kelly suggested. "Will do," Charisse agreed.

The twosome trekked southeast through Manhattan until the beautiful Statue of liberty was in sight. They purchased boat tour tickets and then sat down nearby to enjoy the view as they had an hour to kill before the next boat left. "So, tell me, objectively, how is my son doing? We are concerned about him giving up his legal career to pursue dancing professionally. He's never made such a big change before," Lisa said. "You know I always give it to you straight. My policy is 'Truthfulness is kindness.' The kid has real talent. The other judges seem impressed with his dancing abilities and his chemistry with his partner. I think they're going to pass the auditions, but you didn't hear it from me," Charisse responded. "My lips are sealed," Kelly obliged, and she couldn't hide the smile forming across her face like a rainbow across the sky after a storm. "Oh my, look at that adorable puppy," Kelly pointed out. "Speaking of your son's dancing partner…," Charisse said before Kelly cut her off. "Is that Amelia? The girl with the dog?" Kelly asked. "It appears to be so," Charisse responded. They walked over to greet Amelia and meet her Ballare.

"Oh, my goodness, hello!" Amelia said as she was feeling surprised and startled. Her hands quivered and Ballare fell out of her grip. Ballare jumped up on Kelly and Charisse while letting out short, friendly barks. Ballare was much more receptive to women than men. Kelly picked Ballare up and her face became covered in dog licks. "Ballare is a licker, as you can see," Amelia explained. "That's adorable! I've always wanted a dog; I love them and look at those beautiful eyes!" Charisse said adoringly. As if she was able to understand the English language, Ballare then jumped on Charisse and started licking her, as if to thank her for such an exquisite compliment. "She didn't take too kindly to your son Patrick when they first met. In fact, I recall she drew blood," Amelia said to Lisa. "Patrick hasn't had a dog since our beloved family dog, Brody, passed away. They had a special bond. I don't think he has been able to gather the courage to get a dog of his own, but he does love animals," Lisa responded. "Totally understandable. Ballare is my first and only dog," Amelia said. "Does Ballare like it here by the water?" Charisse asked. "Yes, in fact, it is our thinking spot. What are you doing here?" Amelia asked. "It's Kelly's last day in town. We are about to hop on a boat to tour the Statue of Liberty. In fact, I see it docking right now," Charisse responded. "We'd better go catch our boat, it has been lovely seeing you and I wish you and my son the best of luck," Kelly said. "See you at auditions on Monday! Best of luck!" Charisse added. They boarded the boat and Amelia watched as the boat sailed further and further out to sea.

"You think she cares for my son?" Kelly asked Charisse. "It seems they both are googly-eyed for each other," Charisse responded. "If she's nothing like Veronica, I would be absolutely over the moon," responded Kelly. They both smiled in silence.

Chapter 13: Final Audition

Patrick woke up on a sunny, but chilly city morning. Everything seemed a little fuzzy as he got out of bed. He felt at ease, with an unexplained smile on his face. He heard a knock on his door. He quickly dressed himself and opened the door. Amelia was at the door with two cups of coffee. She walked inside, put the coffee cups down on the table, grabbed Patrick by the shirt and kissed him. Before Patrick had the chance to react, the sound of more knocks on his door interrupted the sweet moment. Patrick walked towards the door, and before he could answer it, Veronica pushed herself in with two coffee cups in her hand. "Hi hunny, I've missed you," she said. "No!" Patrick protested, but the words did not escape his mouth.

Patrick opened his eyes at the first ray of sunshine beaming through the slight opening in his drapes. The first thought that came to mind was how real the dream seemed to be. It was like one of those dreams when you are trying to say something important, but nothing is coming out of your mouth, and you get so frustrated right before you are jerked awake. Another mysterious knock on his door. *Oh no, not again,* Patrick whispered to himself. He pinched his wrist to make sure he was awake this time.

"Hi sweetheart, have you missed me?" Kelly asked. She continued, "I brought you your favorite coffee for good luck before your final audition today. I'm headed back to Boston." Patrick accepted the good luck coffee. "Thanks mom. I haven't had the best night's sleep," he responded. Kelly pinched Patrick's cheek. "You have such nice color in your cheek," she observed. Patrick turned his cheek away. There was no worse pain than a cheek pinch from Kelly. "Is that sweet girl I met putting color in your cheeks?" Kelly teased. Patrick rolled his eyes. "You better pass the final audition sweetheart! Don't mess this up! You're going to pass the auditions!" Kelly said before she left.

Thank you for the gentle words of encouragement, Patrick sarcastically murmured to himself. And then his mind shifted back to his dream. *What a nightmare,* he thought to himself. It was the first time in a while that Veronica popped into his mind, consciously or subconsciously. It was also the first time that he dreamt of kissing Amelia. *What is my mind trying to tell me?* Patrick asked himself, as confused as ever. *Never mind that, I must focus on final auditions,* he redirected himself.

Patrick's performance today, and the results, signified a culmination of all of Patrick's hard work, decision making, and his courage to leave his father's legacy, as well as Veronica, behind. It meant everything to him. The dream/nightmare, at best, served as a distraction for Patrick on this heavy morning.

Patrick had awkwardly spoken to Amelia on the phone one time since the almost kiss, and they decided to meet at the studio early on the morning of the final auditions. Patrick was too timid to ask Amelia to meet for a coffee beforehand. He figured that any communication outside of the competition would put him at risk of being vulnerable. He hadn't been vulnerable to anyone nor put himself out there ever since Veronica stabbed him in the heart.

Patrick arrived at the studio early as promised. The studio was empty. He waited for five minutes and then spotted Amelia walking down the street towards the studio. His heart did a back flip in his chest like an Olympic gymnast. Patrick's eyes began to blink, and he grabbed his coffee cup so tight a drop of coffee shot up through the small opening on the lid and onto the skin between his thumb and forefinger, causing a shooting pain of heat through his skin. *Oh no, here we go again,* Patrick thought to himself.

Luckily for Patrick, it appeared that Amelia failed to notice the potential fiasco. She was looking down and walking at a swift pace, like a good New Yorker. Just as Amelia looked up, Patrick met her eyes and they simultaneously smiled at one another. Patrick strategically moved the dream/nightmare combination to the back of his mind. Amelia's wind-whipped hair was sticking to her ChapStick, and she kept moving her hair off of her face only for it to happen yet again. Patrick chuckled to himself. They locked eyes until Amelia finally reached Patrick's space. Patrick smelled a whiff of the faint scent of the ChapStick-strawberry mixed with lemon—it reminded him of Zebra gum that his mom used to get him for a treat from the drug store. His mom used to get him it when he was home from school sick and would leave the doctor's office to pick up medication from the drug store in the center of town.

"You're here early!" Amelia exclaimed, attempting to ease the tension. "I just arrived a few minutes ago. My mom showed up to bring me a coffee and say goodbye before heading back to Boston," Patrick responded. "It was so lovely to meet her the other night. I'm so nervous,

I didn't even stop to pick up tea on the way here. I had the worst night's sleep," said Amelia. "What a coincidence. I didn't have the best night's sleep either. It's a miracle we're both here. Better yet, no one else had our idea of showing up this early so we have the whole studio to ourselves," Patrick said. "You know why, because a wise man once said you shouldn't study the morning of an important test," Amelia added. "Well, this wise man passed his LSATS after studying the night before and morning of the exam," Patrick said, as he pointed both of his thumbs towards his chest. Amelia grinned. "I get it. I usually cram last minute for my finals. This is why we make a great team," said Amelia. "Now, time to get some dance cramming in!" Patrick joked. Amelia laughed, although the joke hardly made sense. *If you like a boy, always laugh at his jokes, even if they're not funny,* Amelia thought to herself, repeating the advice that her late mother gave her in high school when she experienced her first real crush. Amelia's mother gave the best life advice, and it always stayed with her throughout life. Amelia took her ChapStick out of her purse to reapply and grabbed her purse to look at the picture of her with her parents that she kept in there. It was a small picture they took at a photobooth inside the U.S.S Constitution Museum in Charleston, Massachusetts. Amelia was too young to even remember being there. But she loved the photograph because they all looked carefree and happy, and it also fit in her wallet perfectly.

Amelia and Patrick prepared for the long day ahead of them. They spent the following forty-five minutes using the studio to go over their choreography and dance routine. After they were bereft of practicing, Patrick and Amelia headed to the elevator to the gym upstairs so they could use the locker rooms to shower and change for the actual competition.

As they were on the elevator going up to the 10th floor, they both heard an unexplained, loud, thud and then the elevator came to an abrupt stop. Patrick stayed calm and collected, while Amelia began to freak out. "I guess you're stuck with me forever," Patrick joked. Amelia shot him a blank stare and remained quiet, incapable of even faking a laugh.

She turned away from him, towards the elevator wall and grabbed onto the framed calendar attached to the wall and put her head down. Patrick said nothing more and put his hand on her back. This was the first time he had seen Amelia exhibit fear. *Is it the fear of being late to the final audition or being trapped in this elevator? Think Patrick, think,* Patrick thought to himself.

Patrick pushed the red emergency button near the numbered buttons on the front of the elevator. They waited. Nothing happened. Patrick pushed the button a few more times. They waited again. Still, nothing. The silence lasted a few more minutes, and those minutes felt like a lifetime. *Now what?* Patrick asked himself.

Feeling vulnerable but comfortable with Patrick, Amelia broke the silence. "Now what?" Amelia asked, as if she could read Patrick's mind. "For once, I really don't know. This is an unprecedented situation for me," Patrick admitted. "I could always count on you to be honest at the very least," Amelia responded. "Sorry for acting weird, but this is my number one fear. I used to live on the fifth floor of my dorm building in college and I walked up and down every time to avoid the elevators.

Ironic that I ended up moving to a city like New York, I know," Amelia apologized. "I totally understand. Boston is historically more of a walk-up type of city. The granite underneath is not strong enough to support extreme high-rise buildings. Look at me going off on a tangent. I get nervous when I don't know the answer or don't know what to do next. I always tell corny jokes," Patrick added. "I can overlook the corny joke," Amelia said. "But please get us out of here," she continued. Amelia's hand started trembling. Patrick grabbed her hand and held it. *This feels like home,* he thought to himself. As he looked up, he made eye contact with Amelia. "Promise me one thing, Amelia. If we miss the final audition because of this stupid elevator, no matter what happens, please let's keep in touch. I don't want this experience to be in vain," Patrick said. "Of course, always," Amelia responded. Patrick wasn't sure what to make of that response. Something came over him at that moment, and he pulled Amelia closer and started to kiss her. Amelia jumped and backed away at the sound of a man's voice.

"Hello! Is anyone in there? We're here to help you," a husky voice shouted from outside of the elevator. *Talk about bad timing,* Patrick murmured. What?" Amelia asked. "Nothing, just talking to myself," Patrick responded. "I'm just elated that we are going to get out of here and make it to the audition on time. The comeback is always better than the setback. By the way, did you mean what you said before this mysterious man came to our rescue," Amelia inquired. "Absolutely, of course, 100 percent," Patrick confirmed emphatically.

Hello? Can anyone hear me?" the husky voice asked. "Yes, we are here, please help!" Patrick and Amelia shouted in unison. "This is Arnold. I'm working on construction in the building. I'm going to get you out. Give me some time. I have additional help coming," Arnold responded. Patrick and Amelia covered their ears as Arnold's equipment attempted to pry the elevator doors open. "Never have I heard such a dastardly sound in my life," Amelia said. "I can't hear you!" Patrick shouted. "Never mind!" Amelia screamed, hoping Patrick could hear her.

And just like that, the elevator doors slowly opened. Arnold stood there—a six foot five, muscular man covered in tattoos and wearing a neon yellow construction vest- their savior. "Thank you, thank you, thank you!" Amelia and Patrick recited, as if they had been rehearsing all morning. "Don't mention it," Arnold responded. "If you want to sue the building for this, I can give you a phone number," Arnold said. "That's not necessary, and plus, the judge will never go for it, but thanks again man," Patrick replied. "Sorry to cut this short, but we must get ready quickly to make it on time to our dance audition. We have no time to spare!" Amelia shouted. Arnold nodded and then disappeared into the stairwell.

They got back on the elevator and took it up to the tenth floor—successfully this time. As soon as the elevator opened, they poured out like marbles from a vase. They went to their respective locker rooms, showered, and changed into their carefully selected "winning" outfits. At the same time, Patrick and Amelia met outside of the locker rooms. Patrick looked Amelia up and down in amazement. Not surprisingly, and unplanned, their "winning" outfits complimented each other. Both outfits were black, with hints of blue and a touch of green. "My favorite color is blue, followed by green, and black is always a good backdrop of color," said Amelia. "Blue is MY favorite color. You're copying me as per usual," replied Patrick in jest. "No time to bicker!" said Amelia. They headed back to the elevator and down the studio without any more time to think or worry.

The elevator opened to the floor that the dance studio was on, and this time Charisse appeared. "Geez, you guys look like you've just been trapped inside a tornado," Charisse observed. "It's been a rough morning," Patrick responded. "Is everything okay?" Charisse asked. "It is now. We're all set," Amelia responded. "Excellent. I wish you both the best of luck. Try to relax and remember that you both are incredibly talented," said Charisse. "You're too kind," Patrick replied. "See you in there soon!" Charisse said, and she waved them off.

Patrick and Amelia checked in at the front desk of the dance studio and were given their paper sign with numbers on it to identify them to the judges. Amelia was assigned the number 49, which she considered a sign of good luck. "My favorite numbers are four and nine," she said to Patrick. "I don't have an emotional connection to the number 48, but I'll take all the luck I can get," he responded. Patrick and Amelia were the first partners to perform, and Charisse left the room as she recused herself from judging them due to the potential conflict of interest or appearance of one.

Patrick and Amelia found themselves physically in front of the five remaining judges, but both of their minds were somewhere else completely. True to form, Amelia blacked out once the dancing started. Once her nerves kicked in, she would go elsewhere in her mind while dancing her heart out. This phenomenon has been happening since she did competitive dancing as a young girl. On the other hand, Patrick had a very specific memory that he focused on mindfully right before he had to compete. The memory was a special St. Patrick's Day at the annual

parade in South Boston. Patrick and his mom, Kelly, performed an Irish step dance together. It was the first time Patrick ever danced in front of other people, and it lit him up inside. His father and brother appeared to be proud, and it was one of the best days of his childhood. Patrick visited this memory numerous times as he made the decision to pursue dancing.

Every step, every choreographed move, and every facial expression was carried out assiduously by Patrick and Amelia. After the routine, the looks on the faces of the judges revealed that they all were thoroughly impressed. Amelia's mind came back into the room, and Patrick's sweet family memory faded just in time for them to realize that they were done, they did well, and the judges were pleased. "Thank you for your time, you will be notified of our final decision after the auditions are completed today. Please don't leave the studio until that time," one of the judges said. They thanked the judges and exited the room. Patrick immediately grabbed Amelia, picked her up and flipped her around like they were doing the Tango. Amelia was so relieved and thrilled that she didn't even care. Under normal circumstances, Amelia would be so insecure when someone picked her up because she would think she was too heavy. However, all inhibitions and insecurities had left her body. After Patrick put her down, she then tried to reciprocate by picking him up—unsuccessfully, nevertheless. She nearly knocked him over, but what did him in was him tripping over his own foot. He pulled Amelia down with him. The scene erupted in front of all the dancers anxiously awaiting their turn to impress the judges. The entire room lit up in that moment, and everyone was unleashing roaring laughter. One dancer even spit his water out of his mouth. Patrick hadn't laughed so hard in his life. Amelia couldn't remember a time when she was so playful, goofy and carefree.

Frederick and Dylan were practicing in the corner when they heard loud laughter. They were both surprised when they turned around to see Patrick and Amelia on the floor cracking up.

"What are you two kiddos up to?" Frederick asked them. "It's her fault!" Patrick yelled, and more laughter poured out of his mouth. "I don't know whether to laugh or cry. I'm just relieved that this happened AFTER our audition!" Amelia shouted. "You guys went already?" Dylan asked. "Yup, got that right out of the way," Patrick responded. "Lucky!" Frederick and Dylan shouted together. "When are you two up?" Amelia asked. "We have about ten more auditions before we go. That gives us some time to perfect our moves," Frederick said. "That's why we're friends," Amelia replied. "See you after our audition," said Dylan.

Minutes after the comic relief side show commenced, things were back to status quo in the waiting area. The mood shifted quicker than a dog running after a rabbit. Dancers easily transitioned back to audition mode and nervous looks were once again painted across their faces. In the back corner, Frederick looked uncharacteristically serious and focused, Amelia noticed. At one point, Frederick turned to the wall, along with Dylan, and started praying, hands crossed and all. *What a sight to see,* Amelia thought. "You know, I went to Catholic grade school, high school, and college. I am all 'prayed' out," Patrick noted.

Hours passed while Patrick, Amelia, Frederick, and Dylan awaited the results. Patrick had twenty text messages from Kelly asking about the results. They were all on edge. Frederick and Dylan expressed that they were pleased with the outcome of their audition. After a few hours, the judges announced the end of auditions and asked everyone to come into the front room for the announcement of who passed.

Much to their delight, Patrick and Amelia were among the first names called. Patrick grabbed Amelia and gave her the world's biggest bear hug. Shortly thereafter, Patrick and Dylan sighed in relief as their names were called on the opposite side of the room. Patrick and Amelia were too busy celebrating to heat their names.

The shift in energy in the room was palpable. There was no need to ask everyone whether their name was called --the people whose names hadn't been called—you could see it in their faces. When Amelia saw the gleeful look on Frederick's face. Passing the audition wouldn't feel right if Frederick hadn't passed also. Amelia thought of them as a package deal. Frederick redefined true friendship for Amelia—when you care about someone, platonically, as much as you care about yourself and your own well-being. The friendship was something special Amelia cherished, and it showed. Sometimes friendships formed as adults can be more powerful than childhood best friends. Amelia didn't have many childhood best friends. The dance girls were very clicky and she never felt like she fit in. Frederick welcomed her with open arms and accepted her unconditionally. He was one of very few people that Amelia felt she could be herself around and open up to about

her parents. "He's the ying to my yang," Amelia would always tell people.

Frederick and Dylan ran over to Amelia and Patrick with their hands in the air ready to give double high-fives. Instead of receiving the double high-five from Dylan, Patrick wrapped his arms around Dylan's body and lifted him in the air like a ballroom dancer. Patrick had always been a big fan of the airlift celebratory hug. It was something he learned from his father.

As the group of four was walking out of the studio, Charisse made a beeline to them to congratulate them. "I knew you guys would make it from day one," Charisse said to the group. Patrick couldn't contain his excitement—another airlift celebratory hug was on the horizon—but this time for Charisse. She was caught off guard but accepted it gracefully. Charisse had always been self-conscious of her weight and hated any activity that required anyone lifting her up, such as chicken fighting in the pool. "Let's all go out for drinks!" Frederick exclaimed. "All of us judges could surely use a break," Charisse responded. "I'm in!" Patrick and Amelia yelled in unison. "I as well," added another one of the judges named Monica. Monica was also a longtime acquaintance of Charisse's in the New York City dance world, and they've always had a cordial relationship. "I am observing 'Don't Drink December' but I could really use a diet Coke," Dylan chimed in.

The group of six found themselves at Balade restaurant in East Village squished at a small corner table. "This place has the best middle eastern food in the city and the strongest drinks. I've been coming here since I was a teenager," Frederick explained to the group. "So, tell me more about this 'Don't Drink December' challenge, Dylan," Charisse suggested. "When I'm auditing for a gig or show, I always cut out alcohol, and a theme always helps. I'm hoping to follow this challenge with 'Dry January,'" Dylan responded. "I've never had a 'No Drink' any month," Monica replied. "The only time I went without drinking was when I had to go through the egg retrieval process in my 20s," said Charisse. "Are they for sale? I'd totally pay to have a child with those dancing genes," Frederick inquired. "Patrick!" Amelia yelled in that motherly way she typically scolds him. "No, it's okay. I donated them, right before I moved to New York City," Charisse explained. "Cool!" Patrick responded. "I've always wanted to do that myself, just never found the time," said Amelia. "That's so generous and lovely," Monica added. "Guys, you are too kind, it was really no big deal," responded Charisse. She was too embarrassed to reveal that she got paid for the generous act of service. According to Charisse, every person has an element of deception and telling the truth makes things too irreversible. It wasn't judgement she feared so much as disappointment.

The egg freezing conversation was interrupted by the waiter approaching the table, balancing a tray of drinks on one hand. "Someone sent these over from the bar," the waiter informed the table. Everyone looked incredulously at one another. A lightbulb went off in Frederick's head as he looked towards the bar. He locked eyes with the person he least expected or wanted to see— his father. His father was the person who introduced him to the little known-- best Middle Eastern food ever—restaurant in the heart of East Village. Frederick's demeanor instantaneously transformed. It was rare to see Frederick's more serious side. Amelia was one of very few people privy to it, until this evening.

Frederick's father, Rick, looked at the group and put his own drink up as an air-cheers gesture. The others at the table started to put together what was happening, and it was clear that the fancy man at the bar knew Frederick and whatever relationship they had was contentious at best. Silence enveloped the once noisy table. All eyes were on Frederick, and for once he didn't appreciate it. Amelia was overwhelmed with guilt and empathy. Patrick noticed her furrowed eyebrows and upside-down grin and immediately understood what she was feeling, and what Frederick must be feeling in that moment.

"I'm lost; do we know that man?" Dylan asked. "Frederick does," Amelia responded, giving Frederick the opportunity to clarify to the guy he had a crush on. *Discomfort over resentment,* Frederick used to always say to Amelia, as well as *Honesty is the best policy.* Frederick and his father had a tempestuous relationship at best. Anytime they spoke, words blended into a serpentine hiss. Amelia felt that maybe Frederick needed a little prompt to follow his own advice. Frederick's stomach was in knots, his intestines warring with each other. "That man is my dad, and I do not know him," Frederick responded, reluctantly. All at the same time, the group looked over to the bar where the man was sitting, but he was no longer there. Frederick enjoyed this kind of dysfunctional relationship with his father than the one they had when he was young, invisible, and had a father always ignoring him. Better to believe your life was valuable, under attack, than the alternative.

Chapter 14: Thanksgiving Eve

The holiday season was in full swing in New York City and all the dancers who passed the auditions were joyfully dancing on cloud nine. They would all get to enjoy a quick Thanksgiving break before hitting the ground running with rehearsals throughout the month of December. Yankee will secretly wish all the damned snow would just fall already so this quaint season could get moving into the hedonistic and epicurean pomp that is the Thanksgiving and Christmas season. Frederick, Dylan, Patrick, and Amelia all planned to go their separate ways for the break. Frederick would go as far away from the city and his father as he could, which was London. His mother was spending the holiday in London as well and he loved the decorations that are up the day after Thanksgiving. Dylan, like clockwork, would fly back to Montana to be with his loving family and celebrate the good news with them. Conversely, Amelia would spend Thanksgiving with Ballare in New York City. Her favorite part of the holiday was watching the floats being blown up the day before the Macy's Thanksgiving Day Parade— a very underrated tradition in her opinion. At the other end of the spectrum, Patrick would drive back to Boston to be with Kelly and the rest of his family whom he missed dearly.

The foursome grabbed coffee and breakfast at Mocca Latte's on Wednesday morning, the day before Thanksgiving Eve, which is arguably the busiest travel day of the year. Amelia and Frederick were layered in unnecessary clothing, dramatically shivering due to the drop in temperatures to the 40s overnight after an unseasonably mild Fall season. Patrick was wearing short sleeves and shorts with sneakers. "You guys look like you were ripped from the pages of an L.L Bean magazine. I'm a New Englander through and through," he said, making fun of Amelia and Frederick for wearing several layers and still shivering. "And I'm a westerner through and through," said Dylan, wearing a light jacket, shorts, and sneakers. "We're one in the same," Patrick added. "You guys are not human. Shorts should be outlawed in November!" Frederick said, half joking. The four of them sat there laughing, sipping coffee, tea and eating popovers. It was one of those rare days in the early winter when the sun blazed brightly and the wind held calm, but the temperature was deceivingly low. The trees were beginning to yawn asleep, and the scents of roasted chestnuts carried along the in the brisk air. "It smells like Christmas trees," Patrick observed. "It smells like childhood," Dylan added. Meanwhile, Ballare was in Amelia's tote bag and seemed to be enjoying everyone's company for once. *This is what family feels like,* Amelia thought to herself.

The gatherings at Mocha Latte became a staple for the group after weeks of auditions together. While Amelia already had a Quiet place, Mocha Latte's was becoming her happy place. No one dared to mention Frederick's father's appearance at their celebratory dinner at Balade. Dylan and Patrick departed, sharing a cab for their long trek to JFK airport on the busy travel day. Dylan would be flying out west, while Patrick would be renting a car in the airport and conquering the four-hour drive on his own. Frederick smartly opted for a red eye flight to London later. "Bye!" Dylan and Patrick yelled in unison, and minutes later they were gone. *It seemed like a lifetime ago since we kissed,* Amelia thought to herself, while solemnly watching Patrick leave.

Frederick pulled Ballare out of Amelia's tote. "Come here my beautiful little cutie pie," he gushed. Ballare jumped right into Frederick's welcoming embrace. "You know, you should be honored. Ballare doesn't trust many men in my life. She's just getting warmed up to Patrick, and Dylan she doesn't acknowledge," Amelia stated. "Who wouldn't love me?" Frederick asked. "I certainly do," Amelia replied and gave him a twenty second hug. They learned in one of their psychology classes that a twenty second hug increases oxytocin and decreases stress. From then on, Amelia and Frederick would say "twenty second hug" whenever they were stressed, or happy, or just whenever either of them wanted a hug. Amelia remembered the incident with Frederick's father the other night and figured he might need one, from a human being, although Ballare gives the best dog huddles. "So, do you want to talk about it?" Amelia asked. Frederick knew exactly what she meant. "No," he responded. And that's all he needed to say for Amelia to drop the subject. They had a friendly understanding not to push each other to go too deep. "Are you packed yet?" Amelia tried another, lighter question. "As a matter of fact, I'm not, and I was going to ask you and Ballare to help me. "You know I'm always here if you want to talk," Amelia assured Frederick. Silence followed. Amelia knew that Frederick acknowledged her kind offer, and he didn't need to say anything to convey that to her.

Frederick, Amelia and Ballare made their way to Frederick's humble abode in Tribeca, not without Ballare stopped to mark her territory every two blocks and pulling on the leash to greet every dog and dog owner who walked by. Ballare was the opposite of Amelia: she liked people. Amelia did not appreciate the fake smile she had to put on her face every time Ballare stopped a dog owner; it literally hurt her jaw and caused her to get headaches sometimes.

There was nowhere else like it. Frederick's apartment had a minimalist, naturalistic theme and was painted with dark colors; green and black to be exact. There were abstract portraits of fierce animals decorating the walls. Ballare shrieked when she came close to one of the portraits of a lion, mistaking it for the real thing. Frederick and Amelia chuckled at the adorably naïve moment that only a beloved pet can get away with. Frederick put on an impromptu fashion show which later proved to be pointless as he did not take any of Amelia's recommendations seriously. Amelia had long labeled him "that person who asks for advice only to do what they were going to do anyway." Frederick always responded, "Yeah, yeah, tell it to my therapist." Amelia never liked to talk about her problems to anyone, while

Frederick has been unloading his every thought to a therapist since he was a school kid. After everything was said and done, Frederick's luggage filled the foyer like he was going on a cruise halfway around the world. Ballare jumped into the small luggage that still lay opened on the floor. Frederick kneeled and cuddled Ballare. "I know, I wish I can take you with me, Bally girl," Frederick said with a pout on his face. Amelia rolled her eyes at the cockamamie nicknames he came up with for Ballare. She picked Ballare up and whispered to her, "it's just the two of us and the floats this Thanksgiving." "You're shattering my heart into pieces and filling up my guilt tank," Frederick chimed in. "I have a genius idea. Let's do a Friendsgiving feast with Dylan and Patrick when we're all back in Manhattan on Sunday," he suggested. "That sounds superb," Amelia responded. Ballare barked in agreement. All three of them were on the same page, as usual.

Frederick called a car to escort him to the airport, and that's where their paths diverged. Amelia walked with Ballare in her tote through the decorated streets and to Central Park. Amelia's mind was flooded with thoughts and memories of her late parents during the holiday season. These same thoughts and memories kept her up at night throughout the year but are not nearly as overbearing as they are during the holidays. But for now, on a bench in Central Park, she simply forced her mind to rest and focus on the present. "What should I make for our Friendsgiving feast?" she asked Ballare, not expecting a response. Ballare looked up at Amelia incredulously. If it were up to her, she would choose freeze-dried chicken treats as a side dish. "Let's go to Wholefoods and then make our way to the floats," Amelia whispered to Ballare.

On the other side of town, Charisse headed toward midtown toward Macy's. She loved visiting the floats as they were being blown up the day before the parade.

Charisse walked past a Santa Clause, too skinny, tall and had way too little hair to be the real guy. "Merry Christmas, beautiful," Santa said to her. "Right back at you, Santa!" Charisse responded. Nothing anyone said in New York ever surprised her. She kept walking until she approached midtown. Streets around Macy's were already starting to be blocked off. From afar, Charisse spotted the big, well known, Ronald McDonald float lying on the floor, slowly being blown up. Her favorite float was the Cool-Aid guy. Charisse made her way through the crowd to look for the Cool-Aid guy when she felt a bag hit her from behind and a soft dog bark. The woman whose body the dog and bag were attached to turned around to profusely apologize. "Amelia!" Charisse yelled, surprised to see someone she knew in the crowd. "Charisse! I've never ran into someone I knew at this event! Sorry for hitting you with my dog!" Amelia responded in astonishment. "Do not apologize. Who is this cutie pie?" Charisse asked. "This is Ballare, my little Aussie," Amelia introduced Ballare as Charisse started gently petting her head. "I've come here every year since I can remember. It's so much better than freezing in packed crowds of people on Thanksgiving morning," said Charisse. "I hear you. Thanksgiving morning is for watching the National Dog Show on television with a warm cup of tea," Amelia responded. "I couldn't have said it better myself," Charisse agreed. Ballare put her paw out and touched Charisse's hand. "Oh, that means she likes you, and believe me, she's a tough judge of character," Amelia said. "I'm honored. I've never had a pet or a child, but they all seem to take to me," Charisse joked. "This may seem simplistic, don't judge, but my favorite float is the turkey," said Amelia. "I see it over there! Let's go!" Charisse pointed out. All three of them looked up at the 540-pound, helium-filled Turkey float. "What a sight to see," Charisse marveled at the float. Amelia nodded in agreement.

Charisse and Amelia decided to grab at tea at Starbucks- Mocha Lattes was too far- after they both felt too cold to withstand the weather to see the rest of the floats blowing up. "Brrr. This cold front came out of nowhere," Amelia commented. "You can't take the girl out of Arizona," Charisse joked. They walked into Starbucks and got in the long line. Everyone else must have had the same idea as them. A cold chill infiltrated the room every time someone else decided to walk in. Eventually, when they made it to the front of the line, Charisse and Amelia each ordered green tea with almond milk, while Ballare was gifted with a pup cup. As if it was their lucky day, the pair found a cozy table in the corner that other patrons had just got up from. "Starbucks was my favorite place to go and just people watch when I first arrived in New York," Charisse said. "I love that! Such a great idea!" Amelia responded. "I'm blessed to have met such a great friend like Frederick right away or I would've been so lonely," she continued. "And Patrick. You guys seemed to have clicked right away," Charisse said. Amelia blushed and her true feelings emerged on the surface without saying a word. "I see, Patrick is more than a great friend," Charisse said. "To be honest, I don't know. Promise not to tell anyone, especially Kelly, but we shared a kiss that night after the Karaoke bar. We've been so focused on rehearsals since then," Amelia said, coyly. "Say no more. I'm always here to mentor you if you need it, not that I have the most success with men, but I know what to do, I just don't do it myself," Charisse offered. "Thank you! I'd love a mentor. And I think you do have a way with men. Professor Bryant seems to be quite taken with you," Amelia said. It was Charisse's turn to blush, and she promptly changed the subject. "I'm sure your parents are thrilled and very proud of you. Will they be coming to the show?" Charisse asked. "No, they both passed away years ago," Amelia said matter of factly. "The people we love never really leave us," Charisse responded. Impressed with that logic and insight, Amelia was speechless. "I'm hosting a Friendsgiving Dinner on Sunday. Although you're more of a mentor than a friend, you are more than welcome to join if you're going to be in town," Amelia said gently.

Chapter 15: Thanksgiving Day

Patrick

"Why didn't I just take an airplane. I was at the airport. Why didn't I take the train? What was I thinking?" Patrick lamented to himself. His plan was to hitch a ride with Dylan to LaGuardia airport, rent a car and surprise his family on Thanksgiving morning. It was a wonderful plan, except nothing ever goes according to Plan in Patrick's life. Patrick kicked the tire of his car out of frustration and then yelled out in pain, although his toe was almost numb from the cold snow that got inside his boot and melted into freezing water that turned his toe into an ice sculpture. Patrick was too stubborn to call his family because he didn't want to ruin the surprise. Once he had his mind set on something, he would make it happen come hell, high water, freezing snow, or malfunctioning car.

It turns out La Guardia Airport is not the ideal place to be on Thanksgiving Eve. That's a lesson that all New York transfers would have to learn on their own, and this holiday season was Patrick's time to learn this very valuable lesson. After Dylan parted ways to catch his flight, that's when the plethora of problems started, and everything started to go downhill like an avalanche.

Fast forward a few hours, after the car rental company gave him a sedan instead of the reserved SUV, Patrick managed to get his car to Charlton Plaza, so he didn't transform into roadkill right there on the highway. While Patrick was indulging in a moment of self-pity, he didn't notice the red-haired beauty walking up to him. "Is that you?" she asked. Patrick was startled; he dropped his phone on the ground and looked up at Veronica. *My mind must be playing tricks on me,* he thought to himself. "Veronica?" he asked, in astonishment. It was the word that could escape his lips in that moment. Are you okay?" she asked. "What are you doing here?" Patrick asked, ignoring her question. "I live nearby, I stopped here to get Dunkies and some gas on my way home from work. What are YOU doing here?" Veronica asked. "My tire must have a tear in it," Patrick cluelessly replied. "I meant what are you doing in Massachusetts," Veronica responded. "Right. I'm just visiting for the holiday," Patrick said. "Why don't you call roadside assistance and then come inside and have a coffee with me?" Veronica suggested.

Patrick found himself at a small table at Dunkies with Veronica. The plaza was jam packed with overzealous travelers trying to get to their destination in time for the holiday. "I can't believe we ran into each other like this. How is New York?" Veronica asked. "It's been better than I could ever have imagined. I passed the final audition, and I am slated to be in the show. New York City is wild. Nothing like small-town Boston. Boston is more than a collection of towns than a city," Patrick said. Veronica intervened to put an end to Patrick's indulgent rambling. "Patrick, I've been thinking a lot about you," Veronica started to say. "Hold on, I have an incoming call from roadside assistance," Patrick interrupted, as if he couldn't be less interested in the rest of her thought and barely gazed in her direction. His eyes spoke volumes. Veronica could tell in that instant, his heart was no longer hers, no longer a treasure chest of devotion. "That's going to take too long," Patrick yelled into the phone and let out a grunt, forgetting that he was in public. Veronica heard the frustration in his voice and ceased upon the opportunity to be his savior. "Let me drive you home. You can leave your car here and get it later," Veronica said. Patrick wanted to say absolutely not, but it was a favor he couldn't resist at that moment, at that tiny table for two in Dunkies. *I don't remember Veronica being so generous back in the day, before she knew I would be in a show on national television in the most exciting city in the world,* Patrick thought to himself. He didn't give Veronica a piece of his mind though, he just gave her a phony smile, as he needed the ride to get to his family on time. Veronica was just a means to an end at this time, exactly what Patrick had always been to her. The drive from Charleton plaza to the McDuffy residence couldn't have been more awkward. What do you say to someone who left you at your most vulnerable and then found you stuck in a plaza with car trouble?

Minutes later, Veronica and Patrick arrived at his family home. Like clockwork, they were all there: his mom, family, brother, and some neighbors. His family always started holidays a day ahead of time. He could see them through the big glass window overlooking the kitchen. It was like a scene from a Hallmark Christmas movie, or a Macy's window display. And just like that, Kelly looked outside and made eye contact with Patrick. The next thing he knew, she was running out the front door with arms wide open. *This was a bad idea,* Patrick thought to himself, as he secretly wished he could hop into a time machine and go back in time too before he got in the car and went to the airport with Dylan.

Kelly's face subtly changed demeanor when she saw that Veronica was in the driver's seat of the car. Kelly paused, but it was too late to turn around and pretend she didn't see her. She had a rather bemused look on her face, and Patrick had some explaining to do. Patrick begrudgingly got out of the car and walked over to his mom to do damage control. Much to his dismay, Veronica got out of the car and joined him. "Mom! I came to surprise the family for Thanksgiving. You'll never believe it. I was stuck in the airport almost all-night waiting for a car and then when I was almost home, my tire blew near Charlton Plaza," Patrick explained. "And we miraculously ran into each other," Veronica said. "Well, isn't that serendipitous," Kelly said. "Veronica, feel free to come in and join us. We have more than enough food for everyone," Kelly added. She could not help but to be polite and generous. It was in her DNA. Patrick knew he'd have to cut the trip short, or he wouldn't be able to escape the inevitable, uncomfortable conversation that Veronica had been trying to have with him.

The honey gold glow of the kitchen was quite welcoming, but the people were not. Veronica caught them off-guard. The McDuffy's traditionally ate Thanksgiving dinner in the early afternoon, so Patrick planned to enact his escape in the evening just after dessert. He wasn't picking up what Veronica was putting down and he didn't want to know what she had to say. It was a rather awkward dinner. It wasn't a secret that his brother and parents did not like Veronica, and she lacked self-awareness to realize that her presence was not wanted nor welcome. It was so quiet he could hear the scrapes of the knives cutting the turkey and each piece of turkey being chewed and swallowed. It was so unpleasant that Patrick decided to skip dessert.

Patrick's family understood when he made up an obvious lie. A few snowflakes drifted down from the dark heavy skies. That was Patrick's cue. "The show manager just emailed the dancers, we have rehearsals early tomorrow morning, so I should get going," Patrick lied. "You have rehearsals on Black Friday," Veronica asked, completely delusional to the reality of the situation. "Yes," Patrick coldly responded. All eyes were on Veronica. "I guess I should leave too then. I can drive you back to your car at the plaza," Veronica desperately offered. Kelly interrupted, "Not necessary. I will drive you, Patrick."

Patrick couldn't wait to get to his rental car and call Amelia on Bluetooth. He wanted to tell her about the entire fiasco, while leaving out some pertinent details about Veronica.

Dylan

After numerous delays at the airport, missed connections and a time zone change, Dylan ultimately made it to Glacier Park International Airport. As he followed the signs to baggage claim, he noticed in the distance a sign that said "Dylan" and a smile crept on his face.

Of course, his family would make a huge deal from his brief homecoming. He was going to make it a surprise like Patrick did, but he couldn't hold it in. Even if he tried, his family would see right through his Broadway show. His mom, Greta, was a human lie detector test. She was a tough old lady and often helped his father on their ranch. Nothing got past them. Dylan accepted this reality ever since he was a young lad. Dylan was the middle child; he was sandwiched by two sisters. He was the only son and traditionally would be the one to take over the ranch, but his parents were somewhat understanding when he pursued a career in dance in lieu of the ranch. He found out about the auditions in New York City for the New Year's Eve show, boarded a plane, and the rest was history.

The two smiling faces hiding behind the oversized "Dylan" sign turned out to be the faces of his dorky, nerdy sisters, Sarah, and Mandy. The siblings were mistaken for twins on many occasions due to their closeness in age and similar curly, brown locks. They were like the three musketeers. Dylan could've been happier to be greeted at the airport by his best friends. Growing up on eighty acres of property, there weren't many other friend choices available to Dylan. Maybe that's why he went away to college at New York University, while his sisters opted to stay out west. It was a culture shock for Dylan. He both loved and hated it at the same time.

Ultimately, Dylan decided to move back to Montana after graduating college. He gravitated toward New York City again, and he knew his family didn't approve, but were too polite to speak their minds. Dylan felt he owed it to them to come home for Thanksgiving as it would break their hearts that he would miss Christmas and New Year's Eve.

"Nice sign! I spied you girls from a mile away!" Dylan said. "Family hug, little bro," Mandy said, and the three of them embraced. Mandy was the loving, nurturing one out of the sibling bunch. To an outsider, it may have seemed like a made for television Hallmark moment. To them, it was a simple expression of their love that their parents had modeled their entire lives. They walked to the car as Dylan yelled, "All aboard, Mates." Dylan had a secret talent for mimicking accents and doing impersonations of famous people. His favorite was the British accent, and he was an expert at it. He discovered this talent during elementary school when he had to dress up as a British soldier in a play about the Revolutionary War. He injected laughter and joyfulness into people's lives with his random talent.

Dylan's family surrounded the long wooden oak table, while the fireplace blazed in the background and sounds of birds chirping echoed from the bird feeder outside the back door. The household was in full Christmas décor mode. Dylan's mom, Darcy, skipped Halloween, fall and Thanksgiving decorations; instead, she opted to start decorating for

Christmas on November 1st. She was in her element in the kitchen during the holidays. Within 24 hours, she transformed the house into a winter wonderland with Frosty, like from the movie *Christmas with the Kranks.*

As they entered the house, which was nestled in a picturesque corner of the state, Dylan could hear the sizzle of garlic in hot oil splattering and smelled the scent of fresh herbs. His mother always said that cooking calmed her, but he sensed it was more the art of preparing something her children would love and the satisfaction of watching her children gobble down the food as if they couldn't get such a wholesome meal anywhere else but her kitchen. Thanksgiving Day in his household was like something out of a movie, a perfectly choreographed party.

"Before we eat, let's toast to Dylan!" Darcy exclaimed. All the girls raised their glasses. Dylan noticed his father, Ronald, slightly hesitantly, as they briefly made eye contact. His silence said everything, but Dylan didn't hold back from inquiring further. He didn't appreciate his family blightly ignoring the tension between his father and him since he left Montana again.

"Dad, do you have something to say?" Dylan asked, tired of holding back. "Dylan!" Darcy protested. "No, no, it's okay, Darcy. If you want me to be perfectly clear, we are selling the ranch since you are uninterested in taking it over," Ronald responded. "That's too bad because we are here to celebrate my success as a dancer in New York City, and I was really looking forward to your support," Dylan responded, and the disappointment in his voice was palpable. Dylan's mother and sisters knew to tread lightly for the rest of the meal. The only time the family spoke was to politely ask each other to pass various side dishes. Dylan and his father avoided looking at one another as they were both too stubborn to give in and compromise. Their family didn't yell, never raised their voices unless it was to herd the cattle. At the dinner table, that was the closest they came to a family fight. Dylan's mother managed to carefully steer the ship through the waves, and they avoided the storm. She avoided her usual prodding of Dylan's lack of marriage and kids.

Patrick quietly slipped out of the house while his sisters were clearing the table.

Frederick

Frederick never met an airport bar he didn't love. He treated the holidays like a survival exercise and that he endured with gritted teeth and determination. And it was never truer this Thanksgiving eve. He sat there, alone, at the hotel bar, and befriended the bar tender after ordering a single malt Scotch neat, double. "Maybe I'll stop in Scotland," Frederick through aloud. The bartender rolled his eyes and thought to himself what an obnoxious comment from his typical clientele leaving the city in the wee hours of Thanksgiving. Frederick was the epitome of the home-grown New Yorker, a mixture of privilege and neuroticism blended and presented on a flashy platter. "Are you in finance or law?" the bartender asked Frederick. It was a common, yet incorrect, assumption that many people made about him. "Dance," Frederick replied. The bartender rolled his eyes once more. "Stop messing with me, bro," he said. Frederick winked and then continued to slowly sip his Scotch. A quizzical look appeared on the bartender's face. He refused to reveal his name when Frederick pried. He loved to let people doubt him and then prove them wrong. It was the only sport he was every good at, and he got to practice with his father.

One double Scotch led to another double, and inevitably Frederick was slurring his words and pouring his heart to the unsuspecting bar tender. He caused a scuttlebutt at the bar with the other passengers trying to fend off their nerves by having a drink. They didn't take kindly to Frederick interrupting that. Sometimes Frederick's drunken antic made others uncomfortable, and Amelia wasn't there to mediate. It was typically a strange situation: Frederick was at the bar ordering Scotch, while Amelia ordered a hot green tea with some sort of milk substitute. The bar tender would have to leave the bar area to fetch the hot water, and Frederick would give Amelia a hard time. On this night, Frederick is on his own, like when he was a teenager.

Time flew by at the airport, and Frederick didn't know the difference. The bar tender, to his credit, inquired about Frederick's departure time, but there was no getting through to him if your name wasn't Amelia. The room became hazy, people seemed to be nicer, and Frederick felt a surge of exhilaration and his inhibitions escaped his body. He couldn't stop talking to everyone around him and erroneously assuming they wanted to hear what he had to say.

Frederick was too focused on telling the bartender his childhood struggles that he didn't hear his name over the loudspeaker at the airport. "Are you trying to miss your flight?" the bartender asked, and at that, he officially cut him off. "Maybe in a backwards way, I am," Frederick responded, surprising himself at how insightful his drunk alter ego could be. "My parents actually sent me to Christmas camp when I was in grade school, while they jetted off to Europe and hit all the Christmas markets," Frederick continued to spill his guts to the bartender, "So I spent Christmas with a bunch of kids who still believed in Santa. I convinced them all that they were wrong. A few of them cried," Frederick said as he hiccupped. "Yeah, well my parents could barely afford to put presents underneath the tree," the bartender responded furiously. What Frederick wanted to say was that he would've settled for a Christmas tree, minus the presents. Some of his Christmas memories stung like a wasp and others soothed him, like helping his grandma knit stockings to hang over her fireplace, since he didn't get to in his parent's home. His parents hired a professional decorator to put up their Christmas decorations, and above their fake fireplace hung 6 white stockings, with no names across them, bland and void of spirit.

Thanksgiving morning officially arrived, and the bartender walked away to the other side of the bar and tended to other flyers before shouting "Last Call!" Not five minutes passed before the bar was packed up and the bartender was likely on his way home to spend Thanksgiving with his family. Frederick left the bar to find anywhere else in the airport, still open, that would serve him alcohol. It wasn't lost on him that the airport had nearly emptied. There was a family who looked like they were staying overnight, spread out across the floor with blankets, pillows, kids playing video games and adults on their phones.

Frederick looked down at his watch and was suddenly thrust from his drunken stupor to harsh reality. He power-texted Amelia, but knew she wouldn't respond, as he memorized her bedtime routine and knew she would be sleeping in bed with Ballare, phone on silent sitting on the nightstand by her bed. The panic set in quickly, but the feeling of missing a flight wasn't unfamiliar to Frederick. If he was being honest with himself, he wasn't that disappointed.

Amelia

Amelia was awoken by Ballare's paw stroke across her face on Thanksgiving morning. As she does every morning, Amelia grabbed her phone to check any incoming communication overnight as something world-changing may have happened while she was sound asleep. Her eyes were half open when she saw several times coming in from Frederick. "Oh, my goodness, he missed his flight," she said to Ballare.

Amelia's mind took her to dark places when everything around her was cheery and bright. She historically spent most of the holidays in the doldrums. *"Why am I the only one around here that life has tried to flatten?* She asked herself. Her life was a bare Christmas tree, whereas her friends' lives were 10-foot-tall trees decorated with multicolored lights, and dressed in popcorn, garland, and ornaments, small versions of the Rockefeller Center tree. Amelia kept thinking about Rockefeller Center. Her mother took her all the way to New York City from Arizona to see Rockette's Christmas Spectacular when she was a little girl. That was where her dream of becoming a dancer originated. That had never occurred to her before, or maybe it did, and she forgot. Ballare barked and she lost her train of thought. "Oh alright, let me get decent and then I'll take you out. Looks like it's about to snow," Amelia said to Ballare gently, as if a dog could understand the nuances of the English language. If any dog could, it would be Ballare. Amelia suspected Ballare had a higher IQ than most humans.

Amelia gathered some clean athleisure clothes thrown around her apartment, LL Bean coat and Ugg boots. Ballare already had her leash in her mouth and was ready to go. They walked past a nearby boutique hotel and saw a "Tappy Hour" sign advertising an appearance from the Rockette Dancers on Thanksgiving afternoon for anyone needing a break from their family. Amelia wondered when the advertisements would start going up for the New Year's Eve show she was going to be dancing in. Her mind then jumped to the text messages from Frederick the prior night while he was supposed to be on the airplane. She took out her iPhone and started texting him back. No response. She checked his location- they started sharing a year ago- and saw that he was at his apartment. *This is not good, I better go check on him,* Amelia thought to herself.

Amelia started thinking about Patrick and slipped into a scene that could be their future. The sound of her phone interrupted her daydream and at the sight of Patrick's name on her phone screen, her heart lifted. *"Speak of the devil,"* she said aloud before opting not to answer the phone call and letting it ring a few times. It was her lackluster attempt at playing hard to get.

Lost in thought, time stood still, as did Amelia, but she was suddenly thrashed down into the snow as Ballare lunged at another dog who came into her view. It was an adorable, male Yorkie who caused Amelia's downward tumble through a snowman and onto a patch of ice. She nearly got knocked out and looked up to see, out of all the people, Professor Bryant, with his arm out to help her up.

"You really got knocked off your feet there. I hope you didn't hit your head on the ice," he said. Amelia's head felt heavy, the same way it did when she got in a fender bender in Arizona. She immediately felt a headache coming on, similar to a migraine. "Out of all the people in Manhattan, especially during the holidays, you would be the one to catch me as I fall, Professor," said Amelia, clearly a little dazed.

Professor Bryant smiled. "I think you did hit your head. Let me walk you home," he kindly offered. A surge of clarity rushed through Amelia's head. "Where's my dog?" she panicked.

Professor Bryant spent the next thirty minutes searching for Ballare, while Amelia lay on a park bench nearby praying for her migraine to pass. It didn't occur to her that she shouldn't be glaring into her blue light emitting iPhone. She squinted her eyes painfully as she read incoming, obligatory yet entirely unnecessary, "Happy Thanksgiving" texts. Frederick and Charisse were the first to wish her a happy holiday. Frederick had some explaining to do, but she didn't have wherewithal to do so on Thanksgiving morning. She alerted both of them to the situation, and they were both on their way before she knew it, no questions asked.

Frederick arrived, wrapped in layers of Patagonia scarves, wraps and sunglasses to shield the daylight from worsening his hangover. "You look ridiculous," Amelia blurted out. "Ridiculous? I was going for the French style: cynical and chic. Anyway, I need to get a hydration IV so this better be quick," was the first thing Frederick said when he arrived at Ameli's bench. "I'm the one who needs an IV. I feel like I've been hit by a brick. And why French style? What about London," she asked. "Poor thing," Frederick sympathized, as he patted her head. "Sadly, this isn't my worst Thanksgiving," said Amelia. "Same. I didn't want to go to London anyway. The decorations and markets don't start until after Thanksgiving, so it would've been a tease," replied Frederick. "Wasn't the point of going to London to be with your mother, Aunt and siblings?" Amelia asked. "No, that was never the point. Keep up!" responded Frederick. "And you missed your flight how?" Amelia continued questioning him. "The more pressing matter right now is where is our precious Ballare gingersnap apple pie," Frederick said in an effort to avoid the line of questioning. He loved to assign seasonal nicknames to Ballare. "Right," Amelia agreed, as she almost forgot her sweet little best friend was out there somewhere on the streets in the midst of Frederick's witty banter. "Enough insistent moping, Amelia. We need to go find your pup," demanded Frederick. When Frederick called Amelia by name, she knew he meant business. She accepted his hand and got up off the bench.

They made it one block on foot before they saw Professor Bryant and Charisse approaching with Ballare in tow. Amelia's heart finally slowed down. *There's no better feeling in the world than knowing your dog is safe,* Amelia thought to herself. So much can change in an instant. Amelia knew that better than most people her age. "Charisse, Professor Bryant! Thank you so much!" Amelia exclaimed. "How did you two come together to rescue Ballare?" inquired Frederick. "I was looking everywhere for him," Professor Bryant started to explain. "And I was coming to comfort Amelia, when I saw what I thought was a squirrel running up a decorative Christmas tree on the sidewalk. We must've both came to the realization that it was Ballare at the same time," Charisse finished his sentence. "Ballare was just a few blocks away hiding in a tree. And that's when I ran into Charisse," Professor Bryant finished his story. "What a coincidence," Frederick remarked as he made eye contact with Amelia. Amelia smiled, but in an understated way that only Frederick could pick up on. Charisse and Professor Bryant presented as high school students who just got caught doing something they weren't supposed to do and trying to cover it up. "This is adorable to watch," Frederick slyly whispered to Amelia. Amelia giggled.

Professor Bryant passed Ballare to Amelia. She received Ballare with eyes wide and arms open. Frederick joined in on the family hug as he considered himself an honorary uncle to Ballare and the only man in his life thus far. "My little gingersnap pooch," Frederick ogled him. "My baby," Amelia gushed. "Our work here is done," said Charisse. "I can't thank you guys enough. How serendipitous that you ran into each other and found my dog," responded Amelia. "I couldn't think of a better way to spend Thanksgiving morning," Professor Bryant stated, always one to make the best of the most trying situations. "This morning beats hanging with the Brits," Frederick said. They all shared a laugh. "What got you so distracted in the first place?" Charisse asked. Amelia suddenly remembered the catalyst that set the entire Ballare fiasco in motion: Patrick's phone call. "Hmm, it must've been a phone call from a friend in Arizona wishing me a Happy Thanksgiving," Amelia lied. "It was very nice seeing you guys. I'm happy that Ballare is safe. Time for me to put my obligatory Turkey in the oven," Charisse stated. "I'm going to finish up my morning walk through Central Park. I expect to see you two at finals next week," commented Professor Bryant. "And I'll see you Sunday for Friendsgiving," added Frederick.

Amelia and Ballare got back to their apartment just in time to watch the parade on television. They watched the final product of all the floats they saw being blown up the day before. After the parade, they watched the Westminster dog show so Amelia can compare all the dogs to Ballare and remark about how much cuter she is. If Ballare was a human, this would be toxic mommy behavior, Amelia always joked with her friends. Ballare, however, didn't mind the nonstop gushing and compliments.

Amelia spent the majority of the holiday contemplating what to do about the whole Patrick phone call situation. *Is it too late to call him back?* she wondered to herself. *"Will it seem too desperate if I call him in the middle of Thanksgiving Day?"* she wondered aloud to Ballare. These are things she would normally be asking Frederick, but he was sleeping his hangover off and making excuses to his family. Meanwhile, both of them were pondering what to eat: Tofurkey or Turducken? Tofurkey, obviously meaning tofu impersonation Turkey and Turducken, meaning Dunkin Donut battered fried Turkey. Both things Amelia and Frederik had attempted during their first few holidays they spent together as students.

Amelia picked up her phone as if she was willing it to dial Patrick's number for her. Just on cue, her phone began to vibrate. It was Frederick and when she swiped, his voice loudly came through the phone, "Tofurkey or Turducken?" he asked. "Definitely Turducken," Amelia answered. "Then I'll stop by the store get a Turkey and be on my way. I'm coming over!" said Frederick. "Good luck with that, and we can't wait to see you," Amelia responded.

Chapter 16: Friendsgiving

Amelia never did end up calling Patrick back. Instead, she opted for a breezy text message confirming Friendsgiving on Sunday. She then sent the same exact text message to Dylan and Frederick. Minutes later, she decided to include Charisse and Professor Bryant. Neither one of them seemed to have an abundance of family surrounding them. Amelia had a heightened sense of other people's loneliness during the holiday season as she was lonely for years after her parents passed. She felt a sense of sadness seeing two middle-aged adults with no real plans for Thanksgiving.

Amelia used Postmates to deliver last minute items for the dinner that would occur in the common area of her building. She rented it out as the gathering grew and her apartment would no longer suffice. She was super careful not to have a repeat of what happened on Thanksgiving Day with Ballare. Ballare was on her best behavior for Friendsgiving. She sensed that it was a stressful time for Amelia and curbed her normally hyper-begging behaviors that she exhibited when Amelia was preparing to have company- which was not that often.

The small kitchen in Amelia's not so humble abode smelled of sweetness and brown sugar, which topped her pecan pie. It was a recipe that gave her a wistful longing for Arizona. Her mother used to make a special pecan pie recipe with pecans from their family pecan tree. The pecan tree had been with their family for fifteen years and could've lived another seventy years had Amelia opted out of selling the family home. Pecan pie is the one sentimental thing about Thanksgiving in Amelia's household, and she looked forward to sharing it with her newfound family in New York City. She made a second pecan pie for her and Ballare to share before the guests arrived. She cut a piece, and it tasted like a slice of heaven.

The timer Amelia set on her iPhone buzzed and she nearly dropped the plate holding her precious slice of pecan pie. She was so lost in the sugar rush dopamine hit that she forgot that she was supposed to be stressed out about the turkey, but the stress that accompanied Thanksgiving Day turkey making escaped her. She was elated and her smile was glowing. Even Ballare was in the best mood. It was an inexplicable holiday joy she hadn't experienced in many years. *The turkey looks good so far, one more hour*, Amelia said to herself.

First thing Amelia did before continuing to prepare the meal was wrap up a piece of pecan pie and wrap it in ribbon to bring to the concierge who allowed her to have use of the common room for free. *You catch more bees with honey than with vinegar*, Amelia thought to herself, which is why she left Ballare behind. She was more bark than bite and never warmed up to the concierge. It was something her mother always said to her. It was also something Frederick said the first time she met him when she felt compelled to introduce herself. Frederick had showed up incredibly late to class, the day of the final, but got away with it by bringing a cronut for the professor. Some students rolled their eyes, but Amelia admired his ability to charm people. She immediately recognized it as a skill learned in childhood for survival, the same kind of skills she had to learn as a very young adult.

"What a generous surprise, Mrs. Amelia," the concierge, David, remarked. Amelia formed a bond with David over time as she lived in the same off campus apartment building since moving to the city. Most people were put off by his dark, moody brow that was unbecoming of him. Amelia saw past it. When he saw Amelia, he had a vast, substantial smile on his face. "I'm having a get together in the common room this afternoon, feel free to stop by later for some Turducken although I cannot guarantee that it won't be burnt," Amelia joked. "I'll make sure to let your friends in without any issue, Mrs. Amelia. All they have to do is mention your name and I'll roll out the red carpet," replied David facetiously. Amelia profusely thanked David and headed back upstairs to her apartment.

Ballare was pawing at the door, creating loud scratching noises, as soon as he heard the elevator open down the hallway, and smelt Amelia's perfume. Her neighbor asked her once if she had a racoon in there. That was the most interaction she had with any of her neighbors thus far during her time living in the building. In fact, David was the only friendly person, but he of course was paid to be friendly. Amelia entered the apartment, ready to be pawed and scratched to death for betraying Ballare by leaving without him. She was immediately inundated with the pungent smell of warmth and spice, and earthy aroma. She gathered the silver utensils and antique plates that were passed down from her parents, and she had not unboxed until that day.

Next, Amelia took the turkey out of the oven and gently patted it down with homemade Dunkin Donuts batter. Ballare licked the delicious batter that slowly dripped down the counter like a leaking faucet of mouthwatering candy. Ballare could sniff out Dunkin Donuts batter from a mile away. Back in Arizona, Amelia used to take him for a ride to Dunkin Donuts to get green tea when she was feeling sad, and the cashier at the drive thru always succumbed to his enticing eyes and gave him a free munchkin. On the other hand, Amelia was too preoccupied to notice what Ballare was up to.

The Turducken went back in the oven to finish soaking up the batter. Meanwhile, Amelia was onto the next side: bacon wrapped brussels sprouts. Prepared in advance, these could coexist in the oven with the Turducken for a while. "Mom, I hope I'm doing it right!" Amelia said out loud. It wasn't often that she spoke to her mom from down below. Growing up, Amelia was mesmerized by her mother when she hosted friends and family on holidays and special occasions. There would be two ovens going at once the day off, and the food prepared in advance days ahead of time. All the while, her mom running around with an apron like a hot mess, up until moments before the guest arrive, she would go upstairs and transform into the most beautiful, elegant woman you'd ever seen. Amelia's job was to always set the table, although she always mixed up the position of the knives and forks, and her mother ended up switching everything around anyway. Place cards were carefully arranged on each setting, and everyone got a gift on their plate, such as an ornament, chocolate or make your own plant kit.

"Where did I put those place cards, Ballare?" Amelia asked Ballare. Ballare looked up with her innocent eyes, helpless, and with no answer. Seconds later, Ballare ran into Amelia's bedroom and jumped on her desk. Amelia followed. "That's right, you're the best, thank you!" Amelia shouted, as she opened her desk drawer and found the place cards. One was noticeably absent- Amelia looked close at Ballare and recognized Patrick's place card strategically hidden in her mouth. "I see what you're trying to do!" she playfully scolded Ballare and pried his jaw open with her hands. *Hmm now where do I seat everyone?* she asked herself. She was tempted to sit near Patrick but didn't want to seem too desperate. Ultimately, she chose the safe option, right between Patrick and Chelsea. She locked Ballare in her bedroom while she started bringing everything down to the common room and set the table with the appropriate cards. She lit a cinnamon scented candle that she made at a make your own candle class she attended with Frederick. The common room smelled like cinnamon, Dunkin Donuts and bacon. *Perfect!* Amelia thought to herself.

Dylan was the first to arrive. He was instantaneously enveloped by the coxy atmosphere and delicious smells from the hallway. Like a true western gentleman, he didn't come empty handed. Dylan had such a winsome personality and Amelia applauded him for it. Amelia always felt like her childlike innocence was lost when she lost her parents. Amelia ran over and gave Dyland a bear hug when she spotted him heading into the common room. Dylan presented a luscious, homemade, sugar beet cake, decorated with red and pink frosting. "This is a staple in Montana. Not sure how it will hold up in the Northeast," he explained to Amelia. "You're too sweet and definitely too humble, Dylan," Amelia gushed. Dylan blushed. "I hope Frederick thinks so," he said. "I don't know how fond he is of sugar beet," he continued, appearing slightly nervous. Amelia brushed the comments off. "Oh please, Frederick and I used to eat days old bagels from the cafeteria on our college campus, I think he will savor a homemade Montana staple," Amelia assured him. "By the way, how was your trip to Montana?" Amelia asked, changing the subject so as to put Dylan at ease.

The question had quite the opposite effect. Dylan sighed. "That bad huh? Sorry for asking," Amelia apologized. "Family stuff, you know," Dylan responded coyly. "Say no more," said Amelia confidently. She knew the feeling all too well. "I can't wait to try this," said Amelia. "And I can't wait to try your pecan pie," Dylan said. "It's pe-CAN, not pe-CON," Amelia corrected him. It was one of her pet peeves. Dylan laughed. "I'll keep that in mind!" he quipped.

A voice interjected, "It's definitely pe-CON." Amelia's face turned as red as a bowl of pomegranates. Patrick stood there, looking like Greek god in Amelia's eyes. It felt like weeks since she last saw him, the days passing by as slow as a train ride from Maine to Florida. "No, it's absolutely pe-CAN," another voice said. All three of them looked back at the door to find Frederick standing with a bottle of wine in one hand and a bottle of Champagne in the other. He immediately sensed the judgement in their eyes. "These are nonalcoholic. Don't judge," he immediately blurted out. "On the contrary, these are most definitely alcoholic," Patrick said as he pulled out a twelve pack of beers from his bag. "I need a drink after the Thanksgiving I had," he finished. "I think we all do," Amelia responded on behalf of the group. "There's beer in my Irish Soda Bread, Dylan, just a trigger warning," Patrick warned. "Thanks for the warning, but considering the Thanksgiving I had, I think trace amounts of beer will not disrupt my No Drink November. Plus, in fact I think I deserve it," Dylan responded.

"Frederick, will you help me get the rest of the side dishes from my apartment upstairs?" Amelia asked. "At your service," Frederick sarcastically responded. They walked through the hallway, past the mailroom and to the elevators together, in defeating silence. "Let's butcher the pink elephant in the room before we return. Do you like Patrick or not?" Frederick asked directly. "Tell me first if you like Dylan!" Amelia demanded. "Not the way this works, and you know it," Frederick backfired. "Fine, yes, I do, there are you happy?" said Amelia. "Fine, I like Dylan!" Frederick blurted out. "I knew it!" Amelia exclaimed. "Keep your voice down!" said Frederick. On cue, the elevator door opened.

"What are you going to do about it?" Amelia asked. "Nada," he responded. We have a show to prepare for." Frederick looked at Amelia like a teacher looked at a student about to misbehave. "And are you planning on doing anything about your adornment for Patrick before the show?" Frederick grilled Amelia. "No!" Amelia defensively responded. "Just making sure," Frederick said, and the elevator once again opened to let them out into Amelia's hallway. Ballare started barking as soon as they exited the elevator, the overprotective cutie pie that she was, just couldn't help herself. She felt betrayed that Amelia left her out of the Thanksgiving festivities. The sound of Frederick and Amelia bickering cheered her up right away.

Amelia and Frederick brought the rest of the Thanksgiving feast to the common room. Charisse and Professor Bryant were there and must have arrived while they were upstairs. "Happy Friendsgiving!" Charisse happily greeted them. "Thank you for having me," Professor Bryant politely added. He handed Amelia a plate of cornbread stuffing. "It was my wife's special recipe," Professor Bryant stated. "Maybe don't mention the wife in front of your new lover," Frederick mouthed to Professor Bryant. Frederick was the best at giving relationship advice but rarely implemented said advice to his own life and relationships. When Charisse started to pick up on the communication, Frederick promptly changed the subject. "Guys, enjoy this meal, because after today we must remain in tip top shape. No more indulgence. No sugar, no carbs, no alcohol!" Frederick proclaimed as if he was hosting *The Biggest Loser.*

Charisse brought pastries from Mocha Joes and a box of dog treats for Ballare. "How thoughtful. She's going to love you for this," Amelia said when she saw the donut-shaped dog treats. "Let's do a toast. Thank you everyone for coming and contributing. Please enjoy. Happy Friendsgiving!" Amelia said, standing in front of her newfound family. "Cheers!" everyone responded in harmony, and with unfeathered fervor. They all chatted and passed around the dishes. Patrick cut the Turducken so elegantly and with such strength that Amelia's desire for him grew even stronger. Amelia did pretty alright on her own but sometimes wanted a man around to do these kinds of things for her, like cutting the Turkey and taking out mounting a tv on the wall.

Frederick knocked the fork on his glass of Champagne. "Now, let's go around, and instead of saying what we're thankful for, let's say how ungrateful we are for our families." The winner with the worst family Thanksgiving story gets to host Christmas dinner," Frederick proposed. "Winner, Winner, Christmas Dinner?" Patrick flippantly asked. "Patrick, thank you for volunteering to go first," Patrick snapped back. "Let's see, where do I begin? I didn't get the rental car I reserved, my car broke down outside of Boston, I ran into Veronica, and my mom invited her to stay for dinner, which resulted in an uncomfortably tense situation which I promptly excited at my earliest convenience, but not before my family expressed disappointment in me," Patrick said. It was diarrhea of the mouth. The room turned silent, and Patrick suddenly realized that he revealed his weakness. "Who is Veronica? Is that the ex you told me about on the way to airport?" Dylan asked. Amelia's hurt immediately sank. She was used to excitement and bad news popping up at the moment she least expected it.

Dylan, feeling sorry for bringing that fact to light, volunteered to go next. "My turn. The tension between my father and I was so palpable that it could've lit our fireplace, and my mom turned a blind eye to it. Suffice to say, I left on bad terms," Dylan shared. "With that being said, I guess my Thanksgiving wasn't too bad since I didn't even make it to the point where I had to face my family, just a judgmental, pesky, airport bartender," Frederick shared. "I need more information," Dylan requested. "Yeah, so I missed my flight to London the day before Thanksgiving, as I was drinking at the airport bar, and the next morning

I had the pleasure of joining the search team to track down Ballare," Frederick further explained. Charisse chimed in to remind him that he was lucky to be able to blow off a paid flight to London during the holidays and Professor Bryant voiced his agreement. "As long as you stop missing my classes," he added.

As you all know, I had a scare and almost lost my precious Ballare. Besides that, we enjoyed watching the floats blow up and I ran into Charisse. Thanksgiving Day was quiet as I don't have a family to disappoint me so there's that," Amelia shared. Thinking of the fact that she missed her family and losing someone she recently started caring about made her doubly crushed. Similar looks of guilt brushed the faces of Dylan and Frederick; guilt for complaining about their family, who were still walking the Earth. Charisse and Professor Bryant had looks of empathy and familiarity across their faces. Those looks faded out and transformed to that of embarrassment when the group inquired as to how each of them spent their Thanksgiving. It was obvious to everyone that they had spent the holiday together, but they all knew better than to prod the woman who just got them on the show, and a professor. "Preparing for my online winter classes now that Fall semester is over," said

Professor Bryant, a terrible liar, yet skilled at uncovering lies, especially Frederick's. Frederick swooped in to save the man from the awkwardness he just inadvertently created. "Buon Appetit!" Frederick cheered. And that they did. But not all enjoyed it. The damage was already done to Amelia once she heard Veronica's name. Any mention of an ex in the picture spoiled her their zest. The rest of the meal was uneventful from the outside looking in, but they were all full of emotion and thoughts running through their heads.

As they were saying goodbye, Patrick lingered around until everyone else left. "Hey Amelia, I wanted to talk to you about something…" She cut him off. "There's nothing to talk about. We were only partners for the auditions anyway and that's over with," Amelia said coldly. "What's wrong?" Patrick asked. "If you don't get it, I can't explain it to you," Amelia responded. Patrick froze, didn't know how to respond, and ultimately walked away without saying anything, careful not to make the situation worse. The next day would start a new season: weeks of painstaking rehearsals, practice during days off, followed by the most exciting opportunity of each of their lives, all amid Christmas and then New Year's Eve hustle and bustle.

On his walk back to his temporary home, Patrick couldn't think of anyone to call in the situation except his mother, Kelly. "Patrick I've been worried sick about you!" Kelly cried. "Understood mom, but did you really think inviting my ex to Thanksgiving dinner was a great idea?" Patrick asked sarcastically. "I had no choice. You were the one that brought her to our house," Kelly fired back, never one to back down from an argument, even with her favorite son. "You always have a choice to invite someone to dinner or not! How is not a choice?" Patrick screeched back at her. "So, you've called to yell at your poor mother?" Kelly asked, laying on the guilt thick like peanut butter on bread. The only one who could successfully implement the guilt tactic on Patrick was his mother. His voice softened. "The real reason to call you is to ask for advice," Patrick admitted, and he accepted defeat in that moment. Kelly's toned down her stance. "Tell me everything and I'll help you," said Kelly. "Dylan mentioned the Thanksgiving incident with Veronica in front of Amelia and she seems upset. What do I do?" he asked. "That breaks my heart. Give her some space, sweetie, and then once she's had some time to herself you can swoop in and make your move," Kelly advised. "How much space are we talking?" Patrick followed up. "As much as she needs," Kelly responded. "Great. How unambiguous," replied Patrick. "Good luck, dear!" said Kelly before hanging up. She adopted this version of the Irish telephone goodbye from Patrick's grandmother. It's a genius time-saving hack where you end phone conversations abruptly, in a delightful tone so the person on the other end of the phone can't be mad. Patrick's grandmother was notorious for doing this. Patrick disconnected his side of the phone call. *Thanks for nothing, mom. Enjoy your space, Amelia.* Patrick thought to himself.

Chapter 17: Downtown Kitten Yoga

The studio is called Purfect Yoga Poses. Dylan has less than 24 hours to convince Patrick to meet him there and carry out Frederick's plan. And he has to do so during dance rehearsals, while learning brand new choreography for the show in less than a month. *Purfect!* he thought to himself causing a chuckle to escape his lips during the elevator down to his lobby. His neighbor from across the hallway, a middle-aged financial planner with a permanent vein popped out of his forehead, shot him a hypercritical glare. Dylan's chuckle immediately changed into a pensive look. *If only he knew I was about to go to dance rehearsals and then kitty yoga that might send him over the edge,* Dylan thought to himself, and he made sure to keep the chuckle internalized this time around. Instead, he opted to make eye contact with his jolly neighbor along with a gigantic smile.

As soon as Dylan walked into rehearsals and saw Frederick, he knew the pressure was on. "I'm going to wait until he gets here and then convince him in person. I can't work my magic via text message," Dylan quietly whispered to Frederick. "Amelia is good to go; except I have to convince her not to bring Ballare. She thinks he will pass as a kitten," Frederick said. They both laughed.

Minutes later, Patrick showed up. His face looked eager, searching around the room for Amelia, presumably. Amelia was nowhere to be seen, and there was still some time before rehearsals would start. "I know Amelia's purposely coming late to avoid Patrick. We used to use the late-avoidance technique when Professor Bryant implemented pop quizzes. She'll be here. Trust me," Frederick assured Patrick, which immediately embarrassed him. Patrick wasn't used to people reading him so directly. Bostonians were more subtle than New Yorkers. Dylan made a beeline to intercept their conversation and save them both from each other. Frederick excused himself to the bathroom once he saw Dylan making his way over to them. It was like they were doing a dance in perfect harmony.

Dylan pat Patrick on the back. "Hey man, how are you feeling?" Patrick started off with a generic greeting, concealing his true motive. "I slept real well last night. Those beers put me right to sleep. How about you?" Patrick asked. "Fine," Dylan responded, trying to keep it cool. "Hey, listen. Are you free tonight? I owe you for the tab you covered last night," said Dylan. "I suppose so. What did you have in mind?" Patrick asked. "It's like a stretching class, a lot of the dancers are taking it," Dylan lied. "A stretching class?" Patrick asked. He found the suggestion to be quite dubious. "It's something new I want to try. Think about it today during rehearsal. I'll owe you. Plus, some of the other dancers will be there. Charisse suggested it," Dylan begged. "I'll let you know by the end of the day," said Patrick. Frederick must've been able to read his lips because he winked at Dylan in approval from across the room. In response, Dylan shook his head and smiled at himself. Frederick had a way of getting under his skin and cracking him up simultaneously.

Amelia walked into the dance studio at the last minute for the second day in a row. Charisse took note of the last-minute arrivals and took Amelia aside. "Is everything okay?" Charisse asked in a concerned tone. "All good. I'm exhausted from school and Ballare," Amelia lied. "I thought school was on break," said Charisse. "How did you know that?" Amelia asked. Charisse was mortified "Professor Bryant might have mentioned it. I ran into him downtown yesterday," she responded. "Right, I think we mentioned it at Friendsgiving," said

Amelia. She already had suspicions about Professor Bryant and Charisse's budding relationship that they were being so coy about. "You know you can feel free to talk to me about anything within your comfort. I look at all my dancers as mentees. We are all a family now as we work towards putting on this spectacular show," Charisse stated. "Thank you so much. That makes me feel better. I had a little hiccup with Patrick, and I'd prefer to stay laser focused on the show and avoid him until further notice," Amelia explained. "I don't blame you. Guys can be a distraction. And we all need to buckle down the next couple weeks," Charisse agreed. "I'm going to that yoga class you recommended this evening after rehearsals," said Amelia. Charisse smiled at someone who waved hello to her and turned around to see Patrick walking by, then quickly turned back to Charisse. "Speak of the devil and he shall appear," said Charisse. They both chuckled. "Everyone, places, pronto!" Charisse shouted to the group.

Before the dancers knew it, the sun was going back into hiding, and rehearsals were coming to an end for the day. "Hard work makes the day go fast. Make sure you all stretch," Charisse suggested, and the rehearsal was officially done for the day. They all let out a sigh of relief in unison. It had only been three days, and the week seemed to be dragging on. Dancing all day every day wasn't for the faint of the heart, especially with Charisse in charge. She was given the nicknames "Captain Charisse" and "Commander Charisse" by the dancers, and she didn't mind. Some of the dancers saluted her on their way out of the studio; it was all in good fun.

Frederick snuck up behind Amelia. "Oh, my goodness!" she shouted. He caught her off guard, daydreaming, while trying to avoid Patrick. "Relax! I came over to make sure you don't accidentally walk home instead of going to our agreed upon yoga class downtown. You seemed out of it all day. I'm worried your mind is going to wander and you're going to end up in a holdover," Frederick explained. "I don't have a choice now. I already told Charisse I was going," said Amelia. "She's not your mom. You should go only because you already promised me," responded Frederick. "Don't be so needy, Frederick. And let's be clear, I never promised," Amelia bickered. "Moving on, I'm going to need to borrow your extra yoga mat. Ballare has been biting the corner of my mat, and it is now her toy," said Amelia. "Of course, I always come prepared with an extra mat," said Frederick as if it's only natural to carry two yoga mats on your person at all times. Frederick practically dragged Amelia there. "Frederick, why are you being so insistent?" Amelia wondered. "No reason," Frederick responded, playing coy. Amelia rolled her eyes since she suspected he was up to something and not being forthcoming. She decided to continue walking and go along with his charade, curious enough about the end game not to end it right then and there.

Walking in the same direction but a block over, Dylan claimed ignorance as to why they were heading to this quirky yoga class. He wanted to preserve his newfound friendship with Patrick. "It was Frederick's idea," he let slip. "Frederick's going to be there?" Patrick asked, taken by surprise. Dylan had never been skilled at being deceitful. He had that "out west sensibility" that his father always referred to. "Didn't I mention this to you the other day?" Dylan asked back, unconvincingly. "No, no, I don't think you did," Patrick stated firmly. "It must've slipped my mind," said Dylan. Patrick was skeptical but didn't know Dylan well enough yet to interrogate him, so he let it slide.

Fifteen minutes before the start of the 8:00pm yoga kitten class, both parties arrived respectively. Amelia and Patrick locked eyes just before the entrance, and without hesitation, they hugged it out. Dylan and Frederick let out sighs of relief. All four of them laughed. "Quiet down, no talking once you enter the studio, you'll scare the kittens," the yoga instructor scolded. Amelia and Patrick smiled at each other. She formed an unshakable bond with Frederick over getting scolded by Professor Bryant, and it seemed to be working for her and Patrick by this yoga instructor.

Each of them placed their mats side by side to form the back row of the room, furthest away from the instructor, and hopefully out of her sight. The room was quite small and most definitely sweaty. "I'm turning the heat on now, everyone," the instructor whispered. "I thought it was already on. The thermostat reads 90 degrees," said Dylan. "Shh," said the instructor and another fellow yogi. The other three looked at Dylan with laughter in their eyes, but too much fear to make a sound. Dylan felt like a grade school kid again, being scolded by a nun in his Catholic school, and about to be hit with a ruler. Dylan's face turned into stone at that moment.

After all the yogis in class laid on their mats listening to wordless calming music, they were instructed to close their eyes. Once everyone's eyes were closed, the kittens were released into the room, and shortly thereafter, the yogis were allowed to open their eyes again. Dylan unexpectedly let out an "Ahh!" sound and received a disapproving look from the instructor. While he was used to horses and cattle, cats were another story, even kittens. Not a second later, Dylan began to sniffle, and straight away he felt moisture build up beneath his nose. "Oh, dear lord," Dylan thought to himself. He tried with all his might to hold in the sneeze, which made the sound much more raucous as the sneeze escaped his nose. "Choo!" came out of Dylan like a lion escaping a zoo. The entire class gasped. "Was that a freight train?" Frederick emphatically asked aloud, then gave a contrite look at Dylan when he realized he was the origination of the kerfuffle. The sea of yogi eyes momentarily set their gazes on Frederick, before going back to the original culprit: Dylan. The kitten closest to Dylan dodged out of the way like a baseball player trying to steal a base. Curiously, the draconian instructor continued the class without batting an eyelash. She continued going through the poses without a hiccup, until another kitten walked over to Dylan, his nose became wet yet again, and the four of them let out a series of shrieks as Dylan sneezed. Not another moment passed by before the yoga instructor kicked them out of class and banned them from the studio for life.

They hurried down the street together, creating a symphony of cachinnation. "Riddle me this, Dylan. You invited me to a kitten yoga class, yet you are allergic to kittens. What's in those Nonalcoholic mocktails?" Patrick asked sarcastically. "Why didn't you tell me you were allergic to kittens when we came up with this hare-brained scheme?" Frederick asked facetiously. Amelia was too busy trying to catch her breath to chime in. "I've handled almost every type of animal back in Montana and never so much as a sniffle, but kitten yoga in New York did me in. I'll be damned," said Dylan. "First rule of Friendship with Frederick: never go along with his cockamamie ideas!" Amelia explained. "But, in this case, I'm glad you did," added Patrick as he winked at Amelia. Amelia's mind wondered how just one wink could send her heart into a tailspin of flutters. Good thing Amelia turned away, Patrick thought to himself, because his eyes started to flicker like a broken lamp. Changing the subject, Dylan posed a fair question to the group: "How are we going to explain this to Charisse?"

"We're not," Frederick confidently countered. Haven't you ever told a white lie?" he asked, clearly directing the question at Dylan only. "Not that I can recall. I'm always transparent. I get it from my father," Dylan honestly answered. "That's refreshing," Amelia responded without thinking it might come off as a slight dig toward Patrick. Patrick let it slide, he felt he deserved it anyway. It was his opinion that Amelia was allowed a few more body blows without retribution, and that would make things even between the two of them.

While Frederick and Dylan opted for a random late-night smoothie, Patrick took the opportunity to demonstrate some chivalry by walking Amelia home. "So, you find Dylan refreshing?" Patrick teased. "As refreshing as a lemonade by the pool in July," Amelia quipped. "Truce?" Patrick offered. Amelia stuck her hand out and they shook on it. "Nothing like kitten yoga to bring two friends back together," said Amelia. Patrick sent another wink her way: his way of creating an inside joke with someone he considered much more than a friend.

Chapter 18: Jordana

December 2015

As Jordana sat in her office of her law firm, overlooking a scenic 18-hole golf course filled with Saguaro and Cacti-covered mountains, she gazed at the Christmas decorations lining the room with a smirk. She had to make it Christmasy on the inside if it didn't feel Christmasy outside: it was a balmy 70 degrees that day. Her favorite native Arizonian plant was the Coyote Willow, as it had a hint of Christmas color to it. The phone buzzed and yanked her out of her Christmas haze and back into the reality of her law firm. Molly, her secretary, spoke through the phone, "Your favorite client is on the line," she said. Jordana smiled because she knew exactly who it was: Mrs. Chaplan.

Shortly after moving to Scottdale, Jordana was mesmerized by the amount of wealth, but also the amount of tranquility, a mixture she never knew to be possible on the East Coast. After careful consideration, she made the decision to start her own law firm working with wealthy clients in estate planning. The area of law allowed her to make her own flexible schedule, while getting to experience the trappings of wealth from the outside looking in. Jordana was captivated by moneyed people and their profligate lifestyles. She was astonished how much money they would throw at a lawyer to handle their money. The first thing Jordana did after deciding to open her estate planning law firm was to take golfing lessons. In Scottsdale, business was done over 18 holes on the course in a short-sleeved polo shirt. In Arizona, of course, it was always golf season, so business was done all year round, even for the hard-core golfers, even when the temperatures surpassed 100 degrees.

Although Jordana couldn't quite put her finger on it, she always thought there was something different about Mrs. Chaplan than her other wealthy clients. In fact, there was a Mr. Chaplan, but as the wife, she handled most of the communication regarding their finances and estate, something that Jordana found to be uncommon in southern Arizona. Mrs. Chaplan's husband was the owner of Cactus Golf Course in the heart of Scottsdale, and Jordana met her on the course. Shortly after they were paired up as a twosome, they hit it off, and the Chaplans quickly became the first clients at her firm, but most of her dealings were directly with Mrs. Chaplan. Jordana was also given free honorary membership at Cactus Golf Course, where she had access to unlimited tee times all year long. All her clients came with perks, but this was by far the one Jordana treasured the most. Mrs. Chaplan was generous and loved with wild abandon, yet she had a coy elegance about her.

"Send her through to me," Jordana instructed her secretary, Molly. "Hello, my favorite golf girlfriend!" Mrs. Chapman said. "Hello, my favorite cactus cutie client!" Jordana responded. The fact they were amused by each other's nonsensical jokes further cemented their friendship beyond the client relationship. "My daughter, Amelia, just told me she wants to go to NYU when she graduates high school. I need to know everything about your experience there. I don't want my only daughter moving to the opposite side of the country!" said Mrs. Chaplan. "I hate to be the bearer of bad news, but she'll worship it. I staunchly recommend a cross country move to anyone in their formative years to get a fresh perspective on life," Jordana responded, exacting to be objective with her opinion, although knowing that it was not what Mrs. Chaplan wished to hear. Jordana lived by the motto

"The truth is kindness." She made it a point to always tell the truth to her friends and clients, no matter what, and they appreciated it immensely. "Wait until you have one of your own, she will grow up and move away and break your heart," Mrs. Chaplan said, referencing the fact that she constantly tugged Jordana to have a daughter of her own. "That is not happening unless I go to a sperm bank," Jordana responded, a standard response to anyone who inquired as to why she didn't have children or a husband yet. "Fair enough, let me know next time you can make it out to the course," Mrs. Chaplan said, and they ended the phone call on a harmonious note.

Molly walked into Jordana's office. "I couldn't help but overhear part of your conversation. Do all your clients call you for non-estate-related, personal advice?" she asked. "Pretty much. I view them as my west coast family more than my clients," Jordana responded. "Let's do lunch, on me," Jordana offered to Molly, who promptly accepted, as she was a college student from Montana.

Jordana arrived at the office the next day and the look on Molly's face was devastating to Jordana before she even spoke. I received some bad news this morning. I'm so sorry," Molly drearily said. "Sorry for what?" Jordana nervously asked. "Just say it!" Jordana demanded. "Mrs. Chaplan and her husband died in a freak car accident last night. Your business card was in the car, and the detective left a voice message on the office phone. I just heard it when I came in early this morning. I wrote down the detective's contact information for you," Molly blurted out as quickly as she could before breaking down. Molly was a natural empath; Jordana was not, but this hit home. Mrs. Chaplan was family. "Molly that's not possible. I was just speaking to her the other day, she's fine," Jordan maintained. "Call the detective," Molly asserted, head down, and handed the paper with the phone number over. Jordana grabbed the post it, the note shaking as her delicate hand trembled, and she used her other hand to bend down and let the dog down on the floor. Her legs struggled to muster up the firepower to bring her body back up once the dog was set free. Jordana reluctantly dialed the detective's number. He confirmed her worst consternation: Mrs. Chaplan and her husband were gone. She felt as if time stopped during that phone call. Molly took the dog to her office to comfort herself and to give Jordana space.

Jordana went to her office and pulled the Chaplan file. She was on a mission. She pulled out an envelope that said "Amelia" on it in black block letters. Mrs. Chaplan had asked Jordana to give this envelope to her daughter upon her passing, albeit never disclosed what was in the letter, nor did Jordana ask. Jordana never let curiosity get the best of her when it came to her work. She simply executed the documents and prepared the estate as the clients wished, no questions asked.

Jordana waited until the next day to initiate the difficult phone call to Mrs. Chaplan's daughter, Amelia. Jordana was a fervent believer that a good night's sleep could cure any ailment. Jordana wasn't cured of her grief the next morning, but she was in the right mindset to carry out her duties as an estate lawyer. Jordana let out a sigh of relief when the phone call went straight to voicemail. It was not a phone call she was prepared to make and dreaded all night.

Later that night, with the cryptic envelope in hand, Jordana showed up to the home that Mrs. Chaplan shared with her husband and daughter, Amelia.

A woebegone Amelia, daughter and only child of the Chaplans, answered the door. As expected, she looked forlorn and downcast and didn't seem to make note of the envelope when she motioned with her hands for Jordana to come inside. They had met once or twice and knew who each other was, so Amelia wasn't particularly surprised to see her. There wasn't an abundance of extended family around and it broke Jordana's heart to see Amelia alone. After Amelia motioned Jordana to come in and she ran into the home and onto the blanket on the couch where Amelia had been sitting. Jordana spent hours explaining the estate and then presented Amelia with the envelope. Without thinking, Amelia put it in the nearest drawer and went to bed.

Chapter 19: Goodbye New York

The next morning after Kitten Yoga, Amelia woke up to a phone call from Jordana on her day off. "You sound sleepy. It's 6:00am here so I know it's not too early on the east coast," was the first thing she said. "Kind of an odd night, and it's a rest and recover day from rehearsals," Amelia responded. "Rehearsals?" Jordana asked, baffled. "Oh, did I not tell you?" Amelia asked. "Tell me what? You've been too busy to tell me anything!" Jordana complained. "We have lost touch a bit, haven't way?" Amelia agreed. "You're the hot shot in the big city, I'm just a small-town southwestern woman," Jordana joked. They always poked back and forth about their reversal of moves to and from New York and Arizona.

"Anyway, how are you doing kiddo?" Jordana asked. "I auditioned to be a dancer on a whim, and I got the gig, so I've been in rehearsal mode for weeks and today is one of my first days of rest," Amelia explained. "Well, that was a mouthful girlie. I am so darn proud of you. You are certainly thriving," Jordana remarked. "Did you call me just to inflate my ego?" Amelia sarcastically asked.

"I do have an ulterior motive. I hate to change the subject at this moment. I do need to inform you that there has been an astronomical offer on your family home here in Scottsdale," Jordana stated. "That wasn't on my holiday season bingo card," Amelia promptly replied. "I know it seems out of left field, but the housing market is on fire and there's been an influx of people from California looking to buy houses in Arizona for over asking price. This family from San Diego came here on vacation and fell in love with your home. They are looking to move by the end of the year and willing to pay top dollar to make that happen," stated Jordana. "Do I have time to digest this and get back to you?" Amelia asked. "Of course, dear. Do get back to me I a few days. The potential buyers seem to be on an accelerated timeline and lighting doesn't strike twice. Whatever decision you make, I wholeheartedly understand. Sorry to spring this on you," Jordana said, trying to maintain some degree of professionalism even though she considered Amelia family. "I'll go to my quiet place and think about it. I'll get back to you once my mind has been made up. Please email me the details," Amelia requested. "Sure thing. Oh, and give Ballare a big kiss from me!" Jordana responded.

Amelia gave Ballare a long smooch on behalf of Jordana. "Let's go to our favorite quiet place," she said as she picked Ballare up and placed her in the tote beside her bed. Amelia changed from her pajama leggings to her slightly fancier workout leggings before leaving her apartment. "If Lululemon is cult, call me a cultist," Amelia would frequently tell people to explain her legging obsession in a lighthearted way. The truth of the matter was that she hated dressing up, wearing dresses, heels and being fancy. She just wasn't that type of girl, even though some may argue she was brought up in that world in Scottdale. Amelia preferred the actual golf courses to the country club restaurants that the golfers and their families dined at, dressed to the nines.

With Ballare and tote in hand, Amelia made her way further downtown, after getting a large cup of green tea from Mocha Lattes. She made all her important decisions from the comfort of her quiet place, and this situation was no different. She fled Arizona and pretty much avoided all big decisions related to her parents' untimely passing ever since then. This was something that wouldn't just go away when she closed her eyes, and she knew she had to face it head on before the show. That house in Arizona was the embodiment and representation of her once beloved family and happy childhood. Jordana was the only person from her life in Arizona that Amelia kept in touch with, if only by necessity, since Jordana was still handling the estate, and had recommended a realtor to sell the family property, Melinda. Melinda had lived in Scottsdale her entire life, before it was a celebrity and golf hotspot, and she knew the area like the back of her hand, and she knew the residents too. Melinda had been contacted by a family who wanted the vacant home, she called Jordana in haste, who put in a call to Amelia.

Amelia found her favorite bench with the most perfect view of the Statue of Liberty. The dark water was quietly glistening around the statue. After being born in Montana, doing a brief stint in the desert of Arizona, and living in a big city high-rise, Ballare wasn't too fond of the water since she never got properly acquainted with it, and she was nervous anytime she was close to it, although, she made an exception for Amelia's beloved quiet place. "I wasn't prepared for the day I'd have to say goodbye to that home forever, but I think it's for the best,"

Amelia said to Ballare, trying to convince them both it was the right decision, and at the same time knowing she didn't have much of a choice. The costs for the upkeep of the house weren't worth it and there was no end in sight to her NYC adventures. She could hardly remember the last time she visited Scottsdale. Ballare nodded in agreement. Scottsdale was a distant memory already, and Ballare liked Amelia's new friends in the city. Amelia acquiesced in her decision to go along with the sale of her childhood home.

Amelia's deep thought was interrupted by a touch on her shoulder. She assumed it was Ballare but turned around to see Patrick's face smiling at her in admiration.

"Fancy to see you here," Amelia said. "I'm embarrassed to say I stole your quiet place. It was much better than mine," Patrick admitted. "How dare you!" Amelia said satirically. "Are you for real? You are here taking over my quiet place?" Amelia asked more seriously than her previous statement. "I do not joke. I came here just to think. Honestly didn't think in a million years I'd run into you and Ballare," Patrick stated. "Stranger things have happened," Amelia responded. Amelia scooched over to the side of the bench and motioned for Patrick to join her.

Patrick sat down next to Amelia, and Ballare promptly hopped on his lap as if she had known him for a lifetime. "I must ask. Was Ballare jealous when you came home smelling like kittens after the yoga class?" Patrick asked to break the ice. "You know, I didn't ask her, but now that I think of it, she didn't sleep in the bed, so maybe that was her passive aggressive way of getting back at me," Amelia replied, also trying to break the ice and keep up with Patrick's witty banter at the same time. Ballare let out a little whine as if she knew she was being spoken of. "What a smart girl," Patrick complimented. "Australian Shepards do have the intelligence of a three-year-old human being, and I suspect Ballare has the intelligence of at least a teenager," Amelia bragged. "Yes, and you are not biased at all," Patrick said in a playful manner. They both put their hand on Ballare's head to pet her and they accidentally touched hands; a moment that sent a spark through both of their bodies concurrently.

"What did you come here to think about?" Patrick asked to change the subject. Amelia truly appreciated how straightforward Patrick could be at times. It was a sigh of relief not to have to figure him out like a Rubik's cube. As a matter of fact, Patrick was easier than that to figure out, because Amelia's mother taught her how to figure out a Rubik's cube when she was in middle school. She hadn't tried it since her mother passed away. "I might have to go to Arizona. I got an astronomical offer on my family home that would be irresponsible to turn down, and I think it's time to move one. I haven't been there. Sorry to get so deep," Amelia said. "You do not ever have to apologize for opening up to me. I've been waiting for you to let me in," said Patrick. "Thank you," Amelia simply stated, no witty response necessary. "I think you should go if that's what your gut is telling you to do. Hell, I'd go with you if we didn't have rehearsals," Patrick stated. "That reminds me. What am I going to do about rehearsals?" asked Amelia. "Charisse will understand. I'll practice double time with you when you return to get you caught up," Patrick offered. "That's very sweet," Amelia remarked. Patrick winked to cover up his blushing. "I should call Charisse soon because I don't have much time to make my decision," Amelia commented. "I'll give you some space to make that phone call," responded Patrick. He got up from the bench and walked away. "Wait, Patrick!" Amelia yelled.

"Yes?" he asked. "What did you come here to think about?" Amelia inquired. "Nothing much, just needed a quiet place to relax," Patrick lied. Not the response Amelia was hoping for, but too much else was on her mind to overthink it.

Amelia stayed there on the bench for a while with Ballare, as the crowd dwindled down and the sun faded away. She drafted a few texts to Charisse, and then Jordana, and then deleted them all before sending. A pie-eyed, grey-haired older woman came to sit next to Amelia on the bench, uninvited. She started petting Ballare without permission, but with a kind gentleness that disarmed them. Manifestly, the eldritch woman had witnessed the entire interaction with Patrick moments before. "Was that your boyfriend?" she brashly asked. "No not exactly. We were dance partners. That's all," Amelia defensively responded. "Oh, I see, he was here for a while, looked like he might have been waiting for you to appear, don't be so quick to write him off," the lady suggested. "The heart is forever making the head it's fool," she said. And with that, the mysterious woman left with no further comment. Freaked out, Amelia picked up Ballare in haste and power walked down the street as if a coyote was following her through the woods.

Amelia and Ballare made it to the front steps of their building in record time, and the doorman swiftly let them in since he smelled a sense of urgency. Amelia gave an abrupt greeting to the doorman and then headed to the elevator and pressed the up button a bit too many times. She was spooked by the unexplained woman who approached her, while Ballare didn't seem to mind, as long as she was the center of attention among strangers. "Arizona doesn't seem so bad right about now," Amelia said aloud. She retyped the text messages to Chelsea and Jordana, right before pulling out her laptop to book a last-minute, overpriced, cross-country, first-class flight. If she was going to do this, she needed a hot towel and a free glass of champagne on the way there.

Chapter 20: Hello Arizona

"The plane is preparing for its final descent. We should be landing in Phoenix in approximately 45 minutes. The temperature is 55 degrees in Phoenix with clear skies. Thank you for flying with us," the captain announced over the intercom system. Amelia was enjoying her green tea minus the almond milk (apparently first class doesn't offer milk alternatives), a glass of champagne and popcorn chips; a delectable combination that can only be enjoyed from thousands of miles up in the sky. Ballare was calmly stowed in her usual tote underneath Amelia's seat. Amelia gave Ballare a doggy sedative medication combination prescribed by her vet which helped her make it through the flight in such a tiny space.

Amelia was in an especially bright mood when she left the airport. She had the entire row to herself in first class, her luggage came out of the carousel within the first two minutes, and a taxi was waiting right out in front of the exit doors. As the automated exit doors opened their arms for her, she was engulfed by the hot, arid, Arizona sun. It felt like she was entering the dry sauna at her favorite spa, JW

Marriot in Tucson. Amelia was absorbing all of the dopamine, serotonin, oxytocin and gaba she could before she had to do the most unimaginably hard task she could think of, which was finalizing the sale of her family home. During the cab ride from the airport, Amelia turned her phone back on to check on what she was missing and what was happening in the world the past few hours. A text message from Charisse popped up within a few seconds. The text message read, "Sending you my best wishes in Arizona! When you get back be ready to hit the ground running." Amelia was incredibly thankful to have such an understanding coach in Charisse and at the same time worried about making up rehearsals when she finally returned to the city.

All her worries disappeared when Amelia arrived at the front of her family home and exited the taxi. The house was a distant memory for a while, and now it was standing there, in daylight, as real as can be. The property manager Jordana hired had kept up with the landscaping and cacti plants. The house looked like it had been delicately taken care of throughout the past few years. It was almost as if a family still lived there. Amelia pictured herself eating dinner with her parents at the table which can be seen through the large glass windows on the front right side of the house.

Amelia walked up the stone path through her perfectly mowed front yard and into the wooden double doors leading into the foyer of the house, which also served as their coat room. To her astonishment, there was a fully lit Christmas tree with colored bulbs and red garland, just the way she remembered her mom decorated. A strong whiff of freshly baked sugar cookies swiftly traveled up her nose and through her body. She also noticed the Christmas song "Christmas Wrapping" by the Waitresses playing in the background on the record player her father refused to give up even after iPods and iPhones came out. It was her ultimate favorite holiday song of all time.

Amelia walked through the foyer and into the kitchen to find a tray of freshly baked cookies on the table placed next to a note, presumably in Jordana's handwriting. "Lord give me willpower, but not yet," Amelia said while grabbing a cookie for herself. She picked up the note and saw Jordana's almost too perfect, cursive words written with a black sharpie pen. The note read, "Merry Christmas! Enjoy your last Christmas in this home, even if it came a little earlier this year, Love Jordana." Amelia's heart melted after reading the kind note. Jordana was the only one in the world probably who knew how much the holidays in the Chaplan household meant to Amelia growing up and especially now. The Christmas tree in the foyer was of course fake, but it meant everything to her. Amelia called Jordana to thank her. "Promise me you'll spend at least one day soaking up the Christmas spirit in that house before we get down to business tomorrow," Jordana begged over the phone. Amelia acquiesced at Jordana's request.

Amelia opened one of the cabinets in the kitchen and saw a box of organic dark hot chocolate packs, surely another one of Jordana's touches. "Mom must have told Jordana all about me since she knows all of my holiday favorites," Amelia said to Ballare. Ballare's response was a whine/growl combination. "Ralax, she left something for you as well," Amelia said, as she handed Ballare a red and green decorated dog bone she found in the cabinet next to the dark chocolate. Amelia took a pack out, put water in the tea pot and turned on the stove top. Ballare couldn't wait until the water boiled and so she was given her bone and ran to the living room couch with it. "A watched pot never boils," Amelia said as Ballare trotted off. Amelia looked through the living room windows which had a view of the backyard, including the underground pool, deck and tiki bar. The pool was filled with Christmas floats hanging out on top of the water. There was a gigantic Santa, a snoopy with a red hat (coincidently one of her favorite floats from Thanksgiving Day Parade), the grinch, and a colorfully lit Christmas tree. Amelia said aloud, "Merry Christmas Mom and Dad."

The living room had two stocks, one for Amelia and one for Ballare, hanging over the artificial fireplace. Of course, there is no place for a proper fireplace in Arizona. It was something Amelia's mom designed to make the home cozier and warmer. Jordana had told Amelia it was one of the things that attracted the buyers to make such a substantial offer. Whoever the buyers were, they clearly understood who the Chaplans were, and that comforted Amelia. Amelia cuddled up to Ballare on the living room couch with her hot chocolate and ordered her favorite Christmas movie on Netflix, "I'll be home for Christmas" starring Jonathan Taylor Thomas and Jessica Beil. She identified with Jonathan Taylor Thomas' character; being on the opposite coast for college and having a parent pass away. They both fell asleep before the end of the movie.

Ballare woke up and went over to the window to slightly open the drapes and get a dose of the southwest sun. The few sun rays that peeked through the opening in the drapes awoke Amelia next. The television was still on, the Christmas movie playing on repeat somehow. "Ballare, the only other thing to make this feel like Christmas is if it started snowing outside," Amelia chuckled.

Amelia picked her phone up to call Jordana, before hesitating. She turned her favorite Christmas song out, then found the Christina Aguilera Christmas CD that her mom gifted her years ago and added that to the five-disc CD player. She ate cookies for breakfast with hot chocolate, and then gave Ballare a cookie, even know she knew she would regret it later in the day. She went up in the storage room that they created and looked through some old pictures and Christmas decorations. Her favorite was the different Santa Clause figurines. Amelia's mother was obsessed with Santa Clause and collected numerous figurines throughout the house that were strategically placed throughout the house before Thanksgiving every year. Ballare walked in and licked the dust off the Santas one by one as Amelia laid them out on the floor. "This Christmas" by Christina Aguilera was playing in the background by this time. It was the perfect last holiday in the Chaplan home.

Amelia walked Ballare through the sidewalks of the golf course. Amelia's father had used his golf cart to ride her around the neighborhood, and it was one of her fondest memories of him. The golf cart was still parked in the garage of the home and Amelia would keep it if she could only find a way to bring it back to New York with her, but that wasn't practical nor logical. The quiet sound of golf clubs contacting golf balls was like relaxation to Amelia's ears and her own form of meditation. Most of her neighbors growing up were either snowbirds from Seattle or die-hard golf elitists from out east. That being said, she never really formed a bond with any of them, and her only peers were kids or grandkids from the out-of-towners who visited every so often, until they didn't anymore.

Ballare jumped on and scratched Amelia's legs as she spotted the roaming Jovelina, most of whom didn't acknowledge her. Ballare had never seen such creatures on the East Coast. "We're not in Kansas anymore, Toto," Amelia said, a nod to her favorite childhood movie. Walking through the country club gardens on the sunny morning,

Amelia caught wind of nostalgia. It felt like a wave of nausea through her body and a swollen feeling in her throat as if she had poison ivy, she couldn't decipher between nostalgia and depression, nor the physical symptoms. Her cheeks felt hot to the touch and her eyes were watery, years of pent-up emotions exited her body at once. She tried her best to hold back the tears, rubbing her eyes and pretending she had allergies to all passersby. Ballare was the only one who knew that she was faking it. Ballare hurried do her business so they could turn around and go home and let Amelia feel her emotions in peace.

Later that morning, Amelia started feeling better. She dusted off the old golf cart and took Ballare for a fun ride. Amelia's dad had even installed a manual fan attached to the motor that was used to battle the stagnant heat during hot summers. Ballare was sitting in the passenger seat, with her face in front of the fan, and her ears flapping with every gust of air it blew out.

Once they returned home, Amelia put the golf cart in the front of the driveway, attached to a sign that read, "FREE." She knew she had to part with it and at the same time wanted to be generous like her mother always was. Within an hour, she watched from inside the home as a father and young daughter claimed the golf cart. She put on her favorite Hallmark Christmas Movie, "Every Christmas has a Story," through her Hallmark Movies Now streaming service. Whenever she had the time and needed a boost of wholesome, uplifting, love, she ordered a Hallmark Christmas movie from her couch in New York, no matter what time of year it happened to be.

The movie was interrupted when an incoming call from Jordana came through. "How is early Christmas going?" she asked cheerfully. "It feels like that period between Christmas Eve and New Year's Day when you don't know what day it is. When the Hallmark Christmas movies are still 24 hours on repeat on the television," Amelia responded honestly. "Especially when you're living in Arizona, it feels like summertime outside, but inside your house is still a winter wonderland," Jordana completed Amelia's thought. "I'll have my assistant set up the meeting with the potential buyers for tomorrow. Please feel free to enjoy the rest of your 'Christmas' Day. When you get a chance, can you look for the deed to the house in any of the upstairs room drawers? I can't seem to locate it here. I had my assistance tear up the entire records room," Jordana said, feeling guilty that she had no choice but to both Amelia with this. "You've done so much, no worries at all. My parents were so organized I am sure it will be in a labeled envelope somewhere," Amelia responded. The truth was that Amelia hadn't gone upstairs since she had been back home. Seeing her bedroom and her parents' bedroom was too close to home, literally. Now she had no choice. But she could always push it to later and procrastinate. And that's just what she did the rest of the afternoon.

Amelia tried out the Food Delivery scene in Scottsdale. She ordered dinner for Ballare and herself. The last time she lived in Arizona, UberEATS and Doordash didn't exist. Of course, those services were pertinent to survival in big cities, but she was unsure how they fared in golf towns. To her surprise, Amelia found a plethora of options in the area. She ordered a salmon stick for Ballare from Polkadog Bakery. "Who knew dogs could get delivery too, Ballare!" said Amelia. Amelia ordered her favorite Arizona specialties: Sonoran hot dog and fry bread. She couldn't find any food comparable to this in New York, shockingly.

After dinner, Amelia exhausted all tasks, daily living requirements, Ballare dog duties, and was finally left with the daunting reality of having to go upstairs. Ballare feared the steep, wooden, spiral staircase; therefore, Amelia would have to do this without her fur companion. Ballare stayed in her makeshift bed that Amelia put together with several blankets (very thin blankets only in the house since it was Arizona) and made her way up the wooden, spiral staircase. She had left the top floor of the house untouched since the unthinkable tragedy. She spent most nights falling asleep on the couch watching Hallmark movies.

Amelia first checked out the upstairs guest bathroom in the hallway, the first room one saw when one got to the top of the stairs. There were still old shampoos and conditioners left on the handmade shelf in the shower that her dad made; the realtor must've left them thither to make the place seem homier, like some happy family had been living there this whole time.

Next, she walked past her father's office. He would lock himself in his office for hours on end during the evenings and weekends, working after hours, and handling business calls. It was small, with a large wooden oak desk practically the length of the room, and walls full of various educational degrees and awards. There was one picture, it was a shot of Amelia and her mother on a tour boat in San Diego with the most effulgent smiles across their faces. Her father took the picture when they took a family road trip San Diego many summers ago. It was one of Amelia's favorite memories. They took a tour boat from Navy Pier and got to see a view of the city on one side and Coronado Island on the other, along with a narrator explaining the history of the city. The weather was 75 degrees, and the sun was shining just enough to warm them up from the sea breeze. The ephemeral beauty of the sunset took their breath away. As Amelia hesitantly walked into the office, she spotted the sentimental picture still on the bare wooden desk, a representation of her dearest family memory. At that moment, her eyes started tearing up again. What she wouldn't give to be back in San Diego on that picturesque summer day. Amelia's father always said, "The easiest job is a meteorologist in San Diego, the temperature is always 75 degrees and sunny."

The distant San Diego memory evaporated from Amelia's brain like a rain puddle on a hot day as she entered the master bedroom, which once belonged to her parents. Amelia's mother always kept the room immaculate and without electronics. No televisions, phone chargers or computers were allowed in the master bedroom. They had a luxurious canopy bed with too many throw pillows that looked fit for a king and queen. There was a window facing the front of the house, and Amelia's mother slept on the side of the bed closest to the window because she said she always wanted to see who was coming and going. There was another window perfectly aligned so that her father had a view of the sun rising and the golf course as he was getting ready for work.

Finally, Amelia entered her childhood bedroom. She had a princess canopy bed to compliment her parents' king and queen canopy bed. She dived onto her princess bed and reposed there for a moment looking up at the ceiling. Some of the glow in the dark stars she stuck up there survived, but the glow did not. She opened her nightstand drawer to trigger her memory of what could've been left there before she hastily headed to New York. To her astonishment, she grabbed something that felt like paper or a folder and then saw that it was a manilla envelope with her name written on the front with a black sharpie. She heard Ballare barking from downstairs but remained unfazed. The envelope was unopened and had packing tape, keeping it closed at the fold. Amelia was perplexed. She was hesitant to open it as she had a morbid fear of the unknown ever since she got the worst news that changed the course of her life for better or worse. "Rough, rough!" Ballare nagged from the bottom of the stairs. Amelia placed the envelope ever so gently on her bed and went to retrieve Ballare.

Amelia opened the envelope. She was sure she had combed through the house before leaving for New York, but evidently, she either missed the envelope or it was left in her drawer after she moved to New York, which also would be odd since Jordana and the real estate agent are the only people who had access to the house. "This is an enigma wrapped in a puzzle," Amelia said to Ballare. She picked up her phone to text Frederick. "I'm flying to Arizona immediately if not sooner. Do not under any circumstances open the envelope until I get there. There may be anthrax on it," Frederick responded right away; he always had a flare for the dramatics. "Dramatic play was always my favorite center in preschool," he once said to Amelia. Amelia didn't attend preschool, it was not a requirement in Arizona at the time, so that comment went right over her head, as does much of what Frederick says and does.

Amelia answered her phone on the first ring, already knowing who it was on the other end of the line. "I am booking my flight now," Frederick shouted. "Calm down, don't be ridiculous. It's probably nothing. Just stay on the phone," Amelia responded, downplaying her nerves. Amelia opened the envelope and fell silent. Frederick knew enough to maintain the silence on his side of the phone, he knew to contain his eagerness, and he knew that it wasn't good. He was aglow and he was downhearted. The juxtaposition of two such facts seemed to be auspicious. Amelia did not utter a word beyond, "I need to call Jordana." Her pithy remark was all that was needed to bring the conversation to a close. Then, she used one finger to punch the red end call button on her phone, and everything froze, except the timer counting the seconds and minutes of the phone call. This technical glitch sent her into a tailspin of rage, and she threw the phone up in the air with all her might. The phone hit the ceiling and knocked down one of the glow-in-the-dark stars that she carefully stuck there as a child many moons ago.

On the other end of the call, it took everything in Frederick to keep silent. He gripped his phone with all his strength and made sure not to make any sudden movements with his fingers that would accidentally end the call. He was confounded and disquieted. Seconds passed and with the sound of three "beeps" the call officially ended\ and communication temporarily ceased.

"Do you have something to tell me?" Amelia forcefully and sarcastically asked Jordana over the phone, her voice shaking and volume louder than usual.

The tone of her voice was so in contrast to what she had known of Amelia, it was like a demon possessed her body and took over her voice. This frightened Jordana and caused a lump in her throat like her tonsils were swollen. "May you repeat the question with more context?" Jordana asked. She tried to sound professional, but a thousand thoughts raced through her head. She tried to quickly process the thoughts to determine what Amelia was alluding to. She was truculent and abashed. She wanted to be surprised, but deep down she knew what Amelia was referring to. Her heart started racing at the same tempo as her thoughts, and her appetite disappeared no sooner than it came to her at once. "The envelope!" Jordana and Amelia said in harmony.

"Amelia, have I never mentioned this? There was so much going on back then, it must have slipped my mind. Oh, I feel awful. No wonder you're upset. What do you need from me right now? Please forgive me," Jordana pleaded. "Did you know what information was inside this envelope?" Amelia asked. "No, I did not. Your mother just told me to give it to you. I took it over to the house, put it in your drawer, and must've been so flustered that I failed to mention it to you. I feel sheepish. I can't pretend to understand how you feel right now," said Jordana. "I am beyond speechless. I have to go," responded Amelia. Ballare looked up at her with Bambi eyes, while giving her space. Amelia reread part of the letter out loud, to make it seem real. *"Amelia, my dearest sweetheart daughter, there's something I never gathered the courage to tell you for fear it might tear us apart. I spent years trying to create a family, and after years of trying, your father and me together concluded that we would need to go on an alternative route to start our forever family. As a result, we used egg donation and in vitro fertilization. In short, I am not your biological mother, and we do not share the same genes. I do not know much about your biological mother, I am sorry to report. However, you are the most precious, special, perfect, sweetheart daughter and I am so grateful that you came into my life. I love you always."*

Amelia looked up at the poster on her wall of Aaron Hotchner from her favorite show, Criminal Minds, with a quote from one of the best episodes: *Sometimes there are no words, no clever quotes to sum up what has happened that day. Sometimes the day just ends.* And with that, Amelia's head hit the pillow, and she passed out for the night, inadvertently leaving Ballare to fend for herself. She didn't leave Amelia's side all night.

Amelia woke up at 3:00 in the morning, hoping the envelope and the phone call with Jordana were all just part of a rotten vivid dream. She turned over to her nightstand, nearly crushing Ballare, and saw the envelope and letter still there. She sighed and her stomach started aching. The right side of her neck was so sore she could barely move it, from passing out in an awkward position on three pillows. She punched each pillow several times until Ballare hopped off the bed in fear she would be next. She then tore one of the pillowcases open until the buckwheat poured out all over the side of the bed and the floor. Ballare tasted a piece of buckwheat. *Too bitter,* she thought to herself. "No, Ballare! Too much can cause diarrhea and vomiting!" screeched Amelia. She was at once catapulted back into reality and out of her emotional muddle. Upon realizing that Ballare hadn't even ingested one piece of buckwheat, Amelia dropped the pillow and was thereupon put at ease. She gave Ballare the biggest restraint she'd ever had before. "You're my only family now, sweetheart," Amelia whispered in her ear.

They cuddled in Amelia's bed most of the day until they were both hungry enough to motivate them to have to move out of bed and leave the bedroom. Amelia picked up her phone and saw several missed calls from Frederick and Jordana. She signed and put her phone back down. She was marooned and couldn't speak to anyone. Amelia decided to make a picnic basket out of some of the crackers and cookies Jordana left behind and some of the festive dog treats. They headed to Tucson Botanical Gardens. Amelia figured it was her quiet place before she even knew the concept of a quiet place. For a fleeting moment she thought of Patrick, and her life back in New York.

As they were walking through the gardens, a text message from Frederick popped up on Amelia's phone. "You must've forgotten that you shared your location with me, I see that you are in a botanical garden. I know this is where you go anywhere in the country, wherever you are, whenever you need to be alone to think. I am there with you in spirit. I hope it's not too bad, love," the message read. She held her phone out for a few extra seconds and reread the text message in her head. Amelia hated to admit it warmed her heart that someone out there cared about her. "I owe him a response eventually," she said aloud the Ballare. A couple walking by looked at each other and chuckled as it came across that she was talking to herself. Amelia took notice of the chuckle and started feeling insecure. She abruptly put the phone away in her pocket and said loudly, "Ballare, come on, let's go!" She looked up, and the ephemeral beauty of the sunset took her breath away.

On their walk home, Amelia sent Frederick a text with a meme containing her favorite quote: "Unless I am myself, I am nobody" - Virginia Woolf. Under the meme she simply wrote, "I no longer know who I am." She was fastidious in all her endeavors, which is something she thought was passed down from her mother's genes, but it was passed down from some women she never met, who never had the courage to find her. Amelia took a pause right before realizing that her so-called mother had been living in New York City, according to her mother's letter. "How fortuitous, Ballare. Or maybe not. This could either be the best thing ever or my worst nightmare," Amelia said on the way home, contemplating in her head, while processing everything aloud to her best listening companion. Amelia sent a text message to Charisse which read: "I need another day out here in Arizona. An unexpected family situation came up, and I need some extra time to handle it. I promise I'll be on point as soon as I return," As the message sent, a notification on Amelia's phone popped up and alerted her to a text message from Jordana: "Meet me on the golf course at JW Marriot tomorrow at 9:00am. I made tee time for two. There is nothing 18 holes can't solve. We'll go to 36 if we must. Bring Ballare. She can ride in the cart with us." Amelia paused for a minute, pondering whether she ever moved her golf club set to New York with her. Upon second thought, she remembered that they were in the shed with the golf cart. Her parents brought her a golf club set when she was a teenager as a calming offset to high intensity dancing. However, she quickly realized that there was anything but.

"Are we sharing a cart?" Amelia texted back to Jordana. She knew it would put a smile on her face, and it was time to let her guard time before reality set in and she had to return to New York. "Absolutely! See you bright and early on the course," read the response text from Jordana. Golf is nothing if not stressful, but it takes your mind off everything else going on in life, and any problem between two people can be solved over 18 holes, is what my dad always told me. Ballare, are you listening?" questioned Amelia, as Ballare slowly closed her eyes while in a sitting position. No response. "Is my dad even still my dad, Ballare? Ballare started snoring and her head dropped on Amelia's lap like human toddler.

The phone alarm went off at 6:00am and pierced Amelia's ears. She jumped out of bed, forgot what day it was, time, what state she was in, where she was supposed to be going and with whom she was supposed to be meeting. It was that time in the morning when your brain is still booting up and processing. Amelia's mom always referred to this as "morning mind" when one's brain had the most peace and creativity, before turning on any electronics. Unfortunately for Amelia, looking at her phone was the first thing she did in the morning. And there it was, her text message conversations with Jordana and Frederick, proof that it was not in fact, all just a dream.

Amelia did what she did best in highly stressful, emotionally charged, situations: she slipped into her go-to robotic, daily routine, got dressed, and went about her day as if nothing was wrong. So, she did what she had to do to be ready to tee off. It had been years since she practiced consistently, as downtown Manhattan wasn't a hub for putting greens.

"Have a tee-rrific time on the greens!" said the golf pro to Amelia and Veronica. The joke was a vailed attempt to break the obvious tension between the two and not ruin the day for the others they were paired with. They were paired up with two middle-aged women who seemed to be good friends catching up after spending some time apart. You couldn't break the tension with a chainsaw, but Amelia did feel like chopping off Jordana's head with one.

"I'm Heidi and this is Dr. Sandra," the women introduced themselves. "I'm Jordana." "I'm Amelia." They introduced themselves separately, still apprehensive of the situation. "How do you know each other?" Heidi and Dr. Sandra asked in harmony. "What a long story that is. I haven't had my cappuccino yet. We'll tell you in a few holes," said Jordana, saving the morning for the both of them. "What she said," responded Amelia, and then she took a sip of her plain golf course green tea. "Who put sugar in their gas tanks?" Heidi whispered to Dr. Sandra. Jordana secretly hoped they would be paired with others on the course so Amelia could not lash out too much. They got through the first few holes with ease.

It was Jordana's turn. As she went to hit the ball, a Cactus Ren bird flew from behind her and distracted her, disrupting her swing, and causing the ball to launch in the opposite direction than intended. "Why didn't you tell me a bird was coming?" Jordana angrily asked. "Why didn't you tell me my mom wasn't my biological mom?" Amelia asked, and then she froze in horror as she processed the words that escaped her lips. "Whoa, ladies, this clearly isn't about the Cactus Ren," Dr. Sandra intervened. "Please direct your unfounded arrogance towards me," Heidi chimed in, aiming her vitriol at her friend. "I am not the one who has a tremendous affection for my own intelligence," Dr. Sandra replied sassily. The individual daggers were flying across the green like reindeer in the sky on Christmas Eve night. The tension between Dr. Sandra and Heidi matched the levels of that between Jordana and Amelia. "Can we play through you girls?" the one of the men in the foursome behind the group inquired. "We are not girls, and no you may not," they all chimed in together, sounding like a chorus out of harmony. Nothing brings people together like a common enemy. "Let's savor whatever dignity we have left, and finish proceed to the next hole, ladies," Jordana suggested.

The next few holes were silent, and suffice to say none of them made par, and they all rested on their laurels. "It was never about the Cactus Ren," said Amelia, taking an opportune time to open up to the group as they finished up the 9th hole and ate chicken wraps that they ordered ahead at the turn. "Dr. Sandra can help you two. We're still only halfway through this game. She is one of the best psychotherapists in California. She loves listening to people's problems, and she specializes in family therapy," said Heidi. "Thank you, sweetie. And Heidi is one of the best private investigators in New York," said Dr. Sandra. "We fight like cats, and love like dogs," Heidi explained. "We only see each other once a year, living on opposite coasts and all, so you caught us at a time when we are just catching up the past year," Dr. Sandra added. "Golf is the one thing that brings us together every year. Every year we meet at a different course in the country. Soon we'll have been to them all and will have to start playing courses overseas," said Heidi. "Don't give away our age," Dr. Sandra joked. "If I may ask, how did you guys meet?" Jordana asked. "We have been friends since elementary school in Chicago. We both grew up in the Midwest and then moved away after high school. I set my sights out east, and she went west. She went to University of San Francisco, and I attended Columbia," Heidi explained. "How about you guys?" Dr. Sandra asked.

"That's a good question," Jordana replied. "I was a friend of Amelia's mother," she continued. "They did business together. And I'm visiting from New York City, although I grew up in the area," Amelia added. "Where exactly did you grow up?" Dr. Sandra inquired. "Meadowmere Golf Resort, right around the block," Amelia responded proudly. "You can't swing a Fendi purse without hitting a golf course around here," Heidi laughed, a nod to Sex and the City. "Don't let that fool you, by the way, I gave up golfing when I moved to New York, and I've been dancing," Amelia warned. "Oh, I heard you use the same muscles for dance as you do to golf," Heidi reassured her. "Something about being on the golf course could make any group bond," Dr. Sandra indicated. "And it can make you open up quicker than a therapist's couch," Jordana teased. "Then I might be out of the job soon," replied Dr. Sandra. They each chuckled aloud.

"Anyway, we came to work some things out on the course today, so don't mind if we do," Jordana said, pointing to Amelia and herself. "Please, go ahead," said Heidi and Dr. Sandra together like long lost twins. "Why didn't you say anything?" Amelia asked bluntly. "I didn't know the whole story. Your mom didn't want anyone to know apparently; I just did what I was told. When I saw you the next day, at the house, completely broken, I put the envelope in the closest safe spot I had access to and then went to comfort you. It never crossed my mind ever again, until yesterday, of course" Jordana admitted. "She really never said anything?" Amelia pressed for further explanation. "Never, you have my word," responded Jordana. "Some context here, ladies," Heidi interrupted. My parents passed away suddenly, years ago, when I lived in Arizona. Fast Forward to today, and I found a letter in my Arizona house from my mother stating that she is not my biological mother and had some egg donation thing done. Did I mention Jordana is my parent's estate and trust attorney?" Amelia went on. "That's a lot to digest," Dr. Sandra remarked. "And this is the first time we are speaking about the matter in person. I am not only the trust and estate attorney, but I was also a very good friend of Mrs. Chaplan, her mother," said Jordana as she gestured towards Amelia. "This explains a lot," Heidi interjected. "Nothing has changed, your parents will always be your parents," said Jordana. "Everything has changed," responded Amelia. "It sounds like you two are at an impasse," said Dr. Sandra. "How can we help?" Heidi asked. "You can track down my real mom and give both of us therapy," Amelia teased. Heidi and Dr. Sandra looked at each other in disbelief. Amelia and Jordana stood in stupefaction and glanced at each other with perplexity.

The moment felt like it lasted in perpetuity. In reality, the moment lasted about a minute. "Let's play this whole and move on before we hold up the entire course and everyone wants to play through us," Jordana commented. "Let's do it!" they all responded together.

"That's an eagle, Jordana, amazing!" said Amelia, forgetting for a second that she was livid. "I do my best work under pressure, I'm telling you," Jordana replied. "The men behind us are busy with the beer cart girl, now's a good time to talk. Explain that moment," Amelia demanded of Heidi and Dr. Sandra. "I am a trained private investigator for a law firm, and Dr. Sandra is a psychologist. We are just what you two need. And I speak for both of us when I say we'd love to help," Heidi said. "Well, if the shoe fits," said Jordana. "Out of all the people we could've been paired with on the golf course today, we just come across a private investigator and shrink?" Amelia asked rhetorically. "Life is funny like that sometimes," Jordana replied.

"This person probably doesn't even want anything to do with me, I wouldn't know where to start," said Amelia. "We'll help you every step of the way. You have to get back to New York and continue your dance rehearsals. We will be here," said Jordana. "Why would any of you want to help me?" Amelia asked. "Because I owe it to you," Jordana immediately replied. "And we are bored and halfway to retirement," Dr. Sandra chimed in. "It would mean the world to me, I don't know how I'd repay you," Amelia said. "No need!" Jordana insisted. "Purely kind people truly do exist. I guess I became too cynical out east," Amelia noted. "And I lost my cynicism when I moved out west. Funny how things work out," Jordana observed. "Sandra and I lost our cynicism years ago in Colorado," Heidi said.

"This has been the best round of my life. Oh, how I've missed golfing!" Amelia cheered. "Let's grab lunch at the club house to discuss further and exchange information," Dr. Sandra suggested. "You got it," Amelia responded.

After what seemed like the most transformative round of golf in her life, Amelia arrived back at the house and was promptly greeted by Ballare, who was not pleased to be left alone all day. Nevertheless, Ballare jumped all over Amelia and showered her with love as soon as she entered the front door. "What a day, Ballare!" Amelia exclaimed.

She whipped out her phone and sent a text to Charisse letting her know she would be on a flight to New York City the next day. Her next message was to Frederick., which was long owed and overdue: "I have good news, I'm coming home tomorrow, let's meet before rehearsals" the message read. Frederick's simple response read "I LOVE YOU." It warmed Amelia's heart. She contemplated texting Patrick. *I don't know what to say to him. I don't know if he'll understand. He's so close with his mom, Kelly,* she pondered aloud in her bedroom. She opened her drawer and picked up an old sensory ball from her childhood. It was a clear squishy ball that had several tiny bills inside of it and another blue ball with sparkles inside. Their sticky nature caused them to pick up dust and random hair sitting in the drawer throughout the years. Amelia gagged and threw the balls to the other side of the room when she discovered the balls were covered in yuckiness. *I'm just going to do it,* she thought to herself.

"I've missed you, be back tomorrow," the text to Patrick read. Amelia went out on a limb and showed some vulnerability. Charisse was the first to text back: "I can't wait, you have a lot of work to catch up on!" she wrote. No immediate response from Patrick. "Oh well.

Ballare, we must get the rest of this house tidied up ASAP!" Amelia yelled. Then the doorbell rang and knocked at the same time. Amelia ran downstairs and peeped through the front door hole. To her delight, it was Jordana standing there on the porch. "I come in peace. I picked you up a cactus smoothie on the way here. Let's get this place cleaned out," said Jordana. "Get in here with that cactus smoothie you Scottsdale snob," Amelia aptly joked. "I have ample space at my house by the way, since it's just me, so I am more than happy to store anything you can't bring on the plane or don't want to get rid of just yet," Jordana offered. "Can you store a golf cart?" Amelia asked sarcastically. "Actually, I can. I don't have a half circle driveway for nothing," responded Jordana. "You're too kind," answered Amelia. "That's what family is for," Jordana said. Hours of sorting, packing, and discarding went by in a flash. In no time, Jordana was hugging Amelia goodbye as she and Ballare entered the airport to board a plane back to New York City.

Chapter 21: Back to New York City

Amelia and Ballare exited the airplane and pushed their way to the baggage claim section of the airport so they could scramble through their luggage and find their winter coats. They braced for the cold weather as they went through the automated airport doors to catch a yellow cab waiting by the curb. Her cheeks reddened at the touch of frigid wind and snow flurries. "We're not in Arizona anymore, Ballare!" Amelia giggled.

Frederick jumped out of the back of a limo and approached the cab driver in haste. "This lovely young lady and her pup won't be needing your services today, sir," and handed him a handful of cash. "Come with you," he said, and gestured for Amelia to join him in the limo. The inside of the limo was decked out with over-the-top decorations which included a Welcome Home banner, balloons, confetti, noise makers, and even treats for Ballare. "You really went all out, didn't you?" Amelia remarked. "Maybe, we haven't been apart this long since we met. Dylan has been worried about me and suggested that I channel my nervous energy into doing something special for you and Ballare," explained Frederick. "You really know how to make a girl feel loved," said Amelia. Ballare spotted the treats and made a beeline for them at the last minute instead of jumping into Frederick's arms. "Fair enough," said Frederick in response to the apparent snub. "May I pour you a glass of alcohol-free champagne?" Frederick asked. "Alcohol free? Who are you and what have you done with my friend?" Amelia joked. "Since you completely ditched me, I've been spending a lot more time with Dylan. It turns out he's a good influence on me," said Frederick. "That's wonderful. You know I haven't been gone more than a week," Amelia reminded him. "I'm easily influenced, what can I say!" Frederick hit back. "It did feel like a lifetime," Amelia admitted. "How is Patrick doing? I haven't had much time to keep in touch with him," Amelia inquired. "You'll have to talk to him and see for yourself," Frederick said, playing coy. "I have no idea what that means nor do I have the bandwidth to try to figure it out right now. I'm bereft of oxygen at this point," said Amelia, defeated. "I'm sorry, sweetheart, tell me about Arizona," said Frederick. "Well, I played the best round of golf in my life and received the worst news of my life all within 48 hours, so that was fun," responded Amelia. "You need a hug," Frederick said, trying not to push her too hard for the juicy information he so desperately longed for.

Frederick took Amelia into his arms and gave the cuddliest, most loving, twenty-second hug he could imagine. When he attempted to release the hug, a teardrop fell down her face, and he swiftly pulled her back in again. He could tell this was heavier than he anticipated. "Oh, Frederick, my family has been living a lie. I don't know who my biological mother is. It was all a lie. I have no family, no one," Amelia cried. "You'll always have me," Frederick comforted her.

"Where to next?" the limo driver called out as he opened the partition. "Just keep driving," Frederick yelled back. "How many times do I have to tell you? Family are the ones you choose. And I chose you every time," said Frederick. "I chose you, too," Amelia responded. They hugged again, for more than twenty seconds this time. "We need to find your biological mother. I'll dispatch all my parents' resources, although, I must warn you, biological parents are overrated," said Frederick. "That's very bombastic of you Frederick, which is why I love you. I met a semi-retired private detective on the golf course who is going to help me. Did I mention both her and my mother and in New York City?" Amelia blurted out. "You left that those tiny little details out, missy! Who is this private detective? This is starting to sound like a bad lifetime movie!" Frederick protested. "It was a godwink that I even met her. She'll be back in New York City soon and she's going to help me, while I focus on dance rehearsals, which you need to focus on helping me with, mister!" Amelia responded. "Godwink? Did you find God on the golf course in Scottsdale?" Frederick asked. "Sort of, if you want to put it that way," said Amelia shyly. "I would be less surprised if you said you ran into Santa Clause himself out there," Frederick said to add lightness to the moment. "Are you sure my people aren't better than this Heidi person?" asked Frederick. "It's not like that, Frederick! She offered to help and I rather an outsider does the job," Amelia explained. "Fair enough," Frederick gave him.

Ballare barked to make her presence known as she was used to being the center of attention. "That reminds me, driver, please stop by a fire hydrant at your leisure so our adorable puppy can make pee,"

Frederick directed. "He doesn't need a fire hydrant silly, obviously not a dog person," Amelia teased. "On another subject, what is that chunk of gold on your neck?" Frederick asked. "My mom gave it to me a long time ago for Christmas and I found it in the house when we were cleaning it out," Amelia stated. It was like she was wearing her old life on her neck, not ready to let it go just yet. "I wish I grew up spending Christmas in your household. That is delectable. Your mom has the most elegant taste," Frederick complimented. "She sure was decorous and cultivated, everything I am not, which explains why we aren't biologically related," Amelia stated. "Don't say that; she will always be your mother no matter what. You did inherit your golfing genes from your father, though. "You inherited your dancing genes and love for Christmas from your mother," said Frederick. "Speaking of dancing, how much did I miss?" Amelia asked with trepidation. "Don't you worry, dear. We'll get you back on track in no time. Your parents would've been so proud of you," Frederick responded. "Don't say that. Too soon," said Amelia. "Understood," Frederick replied. He knew when Amelia meant business. "Driver, please take us downtown," Frederick requested. "It's time to go back to my only home," Amelia said solemnly. When the driver arrived in front of Amelia's apartment building, she gave Frederick another hug, picked up Ballare and made her way inside the building while the driver assisted her with the luggage. The Arizona chapter of her life was closed, and a new one was about to begin.

Amelia woke up the next morning shivering as the temperatures fell below zero overnight. "Ballare, I don't want to get up and go out there and face the cold, help me!" she pleaded. All she got in return was licks on the face. She got out all her winter gear: scarves, LL Bean outdoor pants, Michael Kors boots, sweatshirts to cover her dance practice clothes during her anticipated bitter walk. She walked Ballare on their usual route with light snowflakes falling from the sky and the streets lit up in red and green decorations. The winter wonderland was quite a sight to see, and a deep contrast to the southeast. She returned home to let Ballare in, grab her stuff, and head to the studio.

Five blocks later Amelia was making her entrance into the designated dance rehearsal studio that she had spent so little time in since passing auditions. Serendipitously, she bumped into Dylan on the way in. "Well, well, well, look what Santa Clause dragged in from the desert," Dylan joked. He was so sweet that she could overlook the corny jokes from time to time. "Ha ha ha or should I say ho ho ho," Amelia responded with a corny joke of her own. "How was golf country?" Dylan inquired. "I was just taking care of some family things. I did get in an amazing round of golf," Amelia replied. "Jealous of you golfing in the middle of winter in the heat while we are working our butts off here in the bitter cold," commented Dylan. "I am so glad to be back in this cold, snowy, wonderland. You have no idea. I hope you've been taking good care of my dear friend Frederick," said Amelia. "Welcome back!" Dylan cheered as he gave her a bear hug and conveniently ignored the reference to Frederick.

A few minutes before start time, Frederick walked in with serious a serious, aloof look on his face. Amelia took note of the oddity but didn't put too much stock in it, being that her mind was in overdrive. "Welcome back!" yelled Charisse as she emerged from the back of the studio. "Thank you!" said Amelia. "You have work to do, girl, but just do your best today. Tomorrow you can do double time after your 24-hour grace period is over," Charisse stated. "I am so ready for it," Amelia said confidently. "That's what I like to hear from my dancers," said Charisse, and then she walked to the front of the room and pressed play on the stereo. The Christmas music remix blared from the speakers in the room. "Amelia, if you can sit in the back of the room and observe for a while. You can join in once you think you can catch on," Charisse advised. Amelia nodded in agreement.

Patrick walked in late and apologized for his tardiness in a very mechanical fashion, serious look on his face, and his gym bag sloppily sliding off his shoulder. Amelia hadn't spoken to Patrick since leaving New York, aside from one fleeting text message. She took part of the blame for that, but something was amiss. Amelia was sure Patrick would reach out to her, check in on her, ask her how she was doing, anything. Amelia's dad once told her, "When you feel something's off, it usually is, those feelings are real." Amelia was nothing if not insightful, and her instincts were telling her something was wrong.

Patrick didn't acknowledge her as he rushed past her and to the center of the room full of dancers. He carelessly threw his gym bag to the ground right past Amelia without any concern or familiarity on his face. *What happened in the few days I've been gone? This shift is inconsequential to anyone but me,* Amelia thought to herself, sitting there on the floor of the studio, when she should have been paying attention to the dancers. She knew better than that, but she couldn't help herself. She couldn't stop herself from ruminating, which was her toxic strait, according to Frederick.

Patrick almost looked up after her threw his bag, and Amelia tried to catch his eyes, to get a glimpse of him, and to confirm the real Patrick she had gotten to know was still in there somewhere. But his blank stare and tired pupils did not stop to meet her glaze, as they had done so many times before. Suddenly, Amelia flashed back Frederick's comment in the limo, the comment that seemed innocuous and unimportant at the time. *You'll have to talk to him and see for yourself,* Amelia repeated Frederick's words in her head. The words weren't so insignificant in this context. Then Amelia remembered back to mere moments ago when Frederick arrived at the studio with an uncivil nature about him, and Patrick the same just moments later. *This is the same way I felt in Arizona,* Amelia said in her mind. *What else could go wrong with this holiday season? This is going to be the worst Christmas I've ever had in my life. Bah Humbug!* Amelia continued to ruminate.

"Amelia," Charisse said loudly, interrupting Amelia's thoughts and stopping the rumination session in its tracks. Frazzled and mortified, Amelia nearly jumped out up from her sitting position on the floor. "Yes," Amelia responded, in a soft voice, trying but failing to sound calm and under control as if nothing was wrong. "Are you okay?" Charisse asked with pity in her voice and demeanor. "Of course, why do you ask?" Amelia stuttered. "The plastic water bottle you're holding in your hand in crushed and your eyes were closed," Charisse whispered, in an effort not to embarrass Amelia further. Amelia looked down at her water bottle; it looked like a dog had used it as a chew toy and water was dripping on the floor. Mortification didn't even begin to describe how Amelia felt at that moment. "Please, take an extra day to get settled here. It was too soon to ask you to come back. Maybe you can do that kitten yoga again tonight," suggested Charisse. "No!" Amelia protested, louder than a whisper. It was an involuntary reaction; the last kitten yoga class she went to was the last time she was with Patrick, and it was the night she realized she had strong feelings for him. "Sorry, you're right. I'm not feeling well. I'll be back to my old self tomorrow. I'll work overtime. I promise I won't disappoint you," Amelia pleaded. "Don't worry, just get some rest," Charisse reassured her. Amelia tripped when she tried to get up, making things incrementally worse, and Charisse offered her hand to help Amelia balance. Amelia begrudgingly accepted and scampered to get her bags, water bottles, and keys. As she walked out the turn, she briefly turned her head around, and at that time she caught Patrick looking at her longingly. She immediately turned her head back to the door and left the studio without any further incident. She walked home with her tail down between her legs like a dog who lost best in show. She walked through the snow, swallowing her pride, like a sick child is forced to take Dime-a-tap.

"I didn't think it was physically possible the universe could make this week worse, but low and behold, I am now completely alone," Amelia whispered to herself when she finally got to her apartment and shut the door. Ballare overheard and barked as if to remind Amelia that she was not, in fact, all alone. "Oh Ballare, I was referring to humans only. I am completely isolated from all other humans at this time, but I am grateful that I have you," Amelia explained. On cue, she received text messages from Frederick and Charisse. Although she appreciated their checking up on her, she was annoyed with Frederick and embarrassed that Charisse witnessed her minor panic attack. Ultimately, Amelia decided to go to the kitten yoga class that Charisse had recommended. Sitting alone in one's apartment in the dead of the winter in a big city can escalate the feelings of loneliness and isolation, so Amelia implemented the opposite action technique she learned in her social work Cognitive Behavioral Therapy class with Professor Bryant. In doing so, she forced herself to get out of the apartment and do something she didn't want to do. *It can't hurt, right?* she asked herself in her mind.

"Welcome to class!" said the yoga instruction emphatically. *Hopefully she doesn't remember me from last time,* Amelia thought to herself. One of the little kittens was not like the others. It was smaller, quieter and had no black spots. It came over to Amelia and stayed on her mat like a magnet on a refrigerator. The little kitten cozied up in a ball on the back end of Amelia's mat as if protecting her like a guardian angel. That made it all the more difficult for Amelia to do her shavasana, but she appreciated the company, and it made her feel less alone. While she lay on the mat, Amelia looked to her side and saw the thermometer; the room was heated to a whopping 110 degrees. "There is a 100-degree difference between outside the doors and inside this room, how wild is that?" said the yoga instructor. Amelia looked to her other side for the neck stretch and saw the back of Charisse's head a few mats down doing her own neck stretch. (sex and the city quote about people just being there). Between the little kitten and Charisse, Amelia felt stupid for pretending to be completely isolated from the world. "And don't worry guys, the cats are fine in the heat, they can survive in the desert," the yoga instructor announced. "So can I," Amelia whispered to the kitten. When they stood up for tree pose, she made eye contact with Charisse and they each nodded in acknowledgement. By the time the class was doing the last shavasana, Amelia was completely exhausted but knowing she made it through the treacherous heat and complex poses, she felt a rush of dopamine and a sense of accomplishment she hadn't felt in a long time. "We did it," she whispered to her new kitten friend. Charisse rolled up her mat and walked over. "In the mood for a tea?" she asked Amelia. "Always," she rapidly responded. "I know the only café in the city that's open this late," said Charisse. "I'm up for it, let's go," Amelia replied. She left the studio with Charisse, but the kitten stayed with her in her mind.

Charisse and Amelia walked down the street in silence, shivering the whole way, and trying to reach their destination as quickly as possible. They eventually arrived at a 24-hour coffee/tea bar, named Philippe's, located in the west village. "This is the hidden gem," announced Charisse. "That kitten was so darn cute," Amelia said, too preoccupied to complement Charisse's secret tea place. "Agreed," said Charisse. "How is everything going?" she asked, changing the subject. "I was given some unexpected news," Amelia said enigmatically. "About the house?" Charisse inquired. "Not quite, more or less about my family in general," said Amelia. "You can tell me. I feel like all the dancers are my children in a way since I never had my own children," Charisse stated. "I don't know why I am telling you this, I may regret it, but I found a letter in my childhood home, the one in Arizona I went to sell. My mom admitted that she is not my biological mother, could never have kids, and used an egg donor to conceive me," Amelia blurted out. "That's rough, I feel your pain," Charisse commiserated with her. "Life is nothing if not rough," Amelia responded. "Agreed," stated Charisse. "I have an idea to cheer you up. The yoga studio I recommended only uses rescue kittens up for adoption. Why don't you go tomorrow to ask if that kitten you fell in love with is still there. I think that would cheer you up," said Charisse. "That's crazy! The yoga instructor is apprehensive of me, I can't do that," Amelia protested. "I'll go with you," Charisse offered. "Really? You would do that?" Amelia asked. "In a heartbeat," Charisse replied. "What about Ballare?" Amelia pondered. "I think you'll find in life that people, even animals, will adapt to any situation thrown at them," said Charisse. "Ballare sure is a trooper," Amelia agreed. "If Ballare loves you, he'll either love the kitten you bring home, or learn to love the kitten in his own time," Charisse said. "You have an answer for everything, don't you!" Amelia laughed. "I'm never at a loss for words. My second-grade teacher said I could see a refrigerator to an Eskimo," Charisse joked.

"My, my, look what the cat dragged in," exclaimed Charisse.

Amelia's head looked up and her stomach dropped. Patrick walked in

with another young lady, who could've passed as Ameli's sister, if she

had one out there; now there was a remote possibility. It wasn't her

sister though, that's for sure, it was Veronica. Amelia knew it from the

way she looked at him, her eyes lit up, and the way their arms brushed

against each other, coupled with the twirling of her hair with her free

hand. It was an "aha" moment for Amelia. Oblivious to the situation,

Charisse waved them over and greeted them. Amelia clammed up, and

Patrick looked like a deer in headlights. Veronica had a big smile on

her face and said, "Hello, nice to meet you!" very politely to them.

Amelia had a fake, forced smile spread across her face, she couldn't

utter any words out of her mouth. Charisse introduced herself. "This is

one of the dancers in the show and our coach," Patrick said through his

teeth. "And this is Veronica," he added as he gestured toward her. *And

this is awkward,* Amelia thought to herself. The rest of their

conversation was a disconnected series of sentences that did not match

the topic of what the other was saying.

That feeling Amelia got when her parents passed away, then again when she read the letter from her mother, came rushing through her body a third time like a ton of bricks. "It's nice to meet you," Amelia mumbled, at the same time Veronica reached out her hand for a shake. Patrick looked like he was eager to mouth something to Amelia, but he stood there, motionless and quiet. Charisse got the sense that something else was at play. Her mind had been so preoccupied with the upcoming show that she failed to recall the times she noticed the chemistry between Patrick and Amelia. She vaguely remembered, in that moment, at the coffee shop, and it all made sense; Amelia's quiet demeanor, the look of shock on Patrick's face, and the oh so oblivious Veronica. It suddenly dawned on her that Amelia was heartbroken.

"Nice to see you guys, but we have to get back to the yoga studio," said Charisse as she tried to abruptly end the moment. She put her arm in Amelia's arm and shuffled her out the door as quickly as she could. When they were back outside, Amelia asked, "Why are we doing back to the yoga studio?" Charisse responded, "Because we are going to get you that cute little kitten and we needed to exit that uncomfortable situation." Amelia tried to look surprised. "Whatever do you mean?" she asked. "I saw the look on your face. Seeing the one you care about with another woman isn't the most pleasant feeling," Charisse said. The mask was off, and the charade was over. Clearly, Charisse knew how Amelia was feeling on the inside no matter how badly she tried to conceal it. "Was it that obvious?" Amelia asked. "I am good at sensing these things," Charisse replied. "Do you even think the yoga studio is still open?" Amelia asked. "Sure, it is, they have a 10:00pm class tonight, and I wasn't lying about getting you that kitten. Someone once told me you don't get what you don't ask for," said Charisse. "My mom once told me, 'Betrayal is the only truth that sticks,'" said Amelia, with her mind still on Patrick. "Well, isn't that the truth," Charisse responded.

They walked the next few blocks in silence as it was too cold for either of them to speak or do anything other than focus on how close they were to a place adequate heating and inoculation from the winter storm. Together, the pair reached the yoga just in time, and before the 10:00pm class started. The yoga instructor looked up from her desk with and then back down, blithely ignoring them, as they stumbled through the door quickly to escape the cold, and rubbed their hands together in unison as if that would warm them up sooner. Unable to ignore them any longer, the yoga instructor picked her head back up again with an annoyed look on her face. "May I help you?" she asked with contempt. "I'm hoping you can. I was wondering if the little kitten, the only one with no black spots, needs a home. I would like to adopt her," said Amelia. "Say no more, you can have that misfit. In fact, she'll probably fit perfectly with you," the yoga instructor responded. "Are yogis supposed to speak like that?" Amelia whispered softly to Charisse. "I don't think so," Charisse whispered back loudly as they both started laughing. "Is something funny?" the yoga instructor asked, clearly livid at this point in the interaction. "Nothing at all, I'm just very happy about adopting the kitten," Amelia said over her giggle, trying to hold it in before she burst like a frozen pipe in a winter house. "And I am thrilled that you are taking him out of my hands," the yoga instructor responded. "Oh, it's a boy! Ballare and I could use a little testosterone in our household!" Amelia exclaimed. The yoga instructor rolled her eyes to that comment without uttering another word.

She walked to the back of the studio where the kittens lived. "I don't know who raised her, but I can't believe they would unleash her onto the unsuspecting public," Amelia joked. "She mustn't like you very much. She's always been very kind to me. Until now that is!" Charisse giggled. The yoga instructor came back to the front desk a few minutes later with the most adorable, misfit, little kitten they ever laid eyes on in their lives. "My new little sweetheart," Amelia ogled as she took him into her loving arms, with nothing else but a zip lock bag of cat nip and a small litter box.

"Let me walk you home and make you and kitten get home safely," Charisse offered, and Amelia promptly accepted. "Thank you for taking my mind off things tonight, I needed it," Amelia said. "You can always count on me to do so, now what you really need is sleep. I want to see you bright and early tomorrow at the studio," Charisse ordered.

Later that night, Amelia laid awake in bed with Ballare and the new kitten, pondering what to name him. "Let me think," she said aloud as she stroked her chin. I want to dance, and I also want courage. "What about Coraggio?" she asked her audience of pets. She took their silence to mean they agreed with her. "I'll call you Coro for short," she said to the kitten as she patted the top of his head. He seemed to take to the name just fine. Ballare was distant yet welcoming with Coro. *It'll be a matter of time before they warm up to one another,* she thought to herself as she watched them sit there quietly at the end of her bed. "We're a little family now," she said to them. They just looked back at her with their sweet eyes. It melted her heart and subsequently put her to sleep.

Amelia only hit the pillow for four hours before waking up at the crack of dawn to check on her new little family. She put Coro in her tote bag and took him along for Ballare's daily morning walk. She put a blanket on him and dressed Ballare up in her winter coat and booties. She responded to the text message from Charisse checking in on the new family member to reassure her that everything was going fine, and the first night together was a success.

The pets were settled in after their walk, Amelia was all bundled up, and the only thing left was for her to get her proverbial big girl pants on, head to rehearsal, and face the music. But first, Mocca Lattes. She made sure to leave her place a few minutes early to make her pit stop to get a green tea and wait in line just in case the Manhattan tree tourists were in town and taking over the coffee shops this year. When she entered and saw that there was no line, she realized she must have misjudged how late the tree tourists wake up when they are spending all night in crowds in Rockefeller Center in temperatures they aren't used to enduring. She did see a couple of familiar faces: Dylan and Frederick.

Frederick zipped by the other customers and made a beeline for Amelia, while Dylan politely stayed back to assess the situation. "You haven't responded to any of my texts," he said worriedly. "Please lower your voice," Amelia whispered back at him. "I've been worried sick about you all night, I even tried to bribe your doorman to no avail," said Frederick. "You tried to bribe my doorman?" Amelia yelled in astonishment. "Now it's your turn to lower your voice," Frederick whispered. Dylan motioned for customers to pass them as they were clearly in the middle of a tense conversation smack in the middle of the coffee shop. He was obviously embarrassed to be associated with them given their public behavior, but Dylan did a good job hiding his embarrassment out of his common decency and loyal friendship. It was also clear that Frederick had grown on him, and he accepted Frederick at his best and worst.

"I know about Patrick. I saw you guys walking into the dance studio, both late, minutes apart. You kept something from me. You betrayed our friendship, and I am deeply disappointed. I need some space, from everyone," Amelia explained. "I don't do space. Not with my best friends. Not with you," Frederick replied. "Frederick! Let me order my tea already or you'll make me late," Amelia demanded. Dylan walked over and handed Amelia an already made and paid for green tea with almond milk. "Why can't all men be like you, Dylan?" Amelia asked as she accepted the tea. "I second that," said Frederick. "You guys are too kind. And you mean too much to me to let your friendship go. But right now, we do need to get to rehearsals," said Dylan objectively. And off they went on their walk to rehearsals together without another word.

Charisse looked delighted to see the trio walk into the studio together and on time. "So happy to hear that Coro made it through the night unscathed!" Charisse exclaimed. "What in the world is a Coro?"

Frederick asked. "Amelia's kitten!" Charisse responded. "Since when do you have a kitten?" Frederick questioned Amelia. Charisse was caught off guard; it was unbeknownst to her that their friendship had fractured overnight, and Amelia hadn't told Frederick about the exciting news yet. She looked at Dylan for clarification, and he shrugged his shoulders as he was just as confused and out of the loop as her. "Anyway, guys, get to your places," Charisse said.

Amelia was focused on keeping up with the choreography, but it didn't go unnoticed to her that Patrick strategically stayed in the back of the room near the door. *How Convenient,* Amelia thought to herself. *I better not make myself look like a fool,* she added. It was a good thing that Amelia had a photographic memory. She nearly memorized the part of the dance routine she watched the other day, until Charisse kindly escorted her out of the studio. She stayed up for hours after Ballare and Coro were settled in bed and practiced the routine in her living room over and over again until she got it down pact. There was no way she was going to let anyone get in the way of her dream. "A dream isn't something you wish for, it's something you work for," Amelia's father used to say to her, and the quote had been ingrained in her mind ever since childhood.

Amelia's mind completely cleared of any thoughts of Patrick judging her, or anyone else for that matter, and joined the group in their routine. Dancing was the anthesis of golfing in Amelia's mind. While golfing, she engaged in deep thinking, heavy discussions, and problem solving. While dancing, her mind was completely Zen and in the present moment without any thoughts besides the choreography, which mostly came naturally to her anyway given her excellent memory.

"Amazing job, Amelia!" Charisse shouted from the front of the studio in between her counting beats and various words of encouragement. Amelia was too entranced with the dance routine to respond in any way except continuing. When the parts of the dance that she didn't get to observe came up, she methodically followed the dancers on either side of her, hoping that she didn't look like a fool.

When she spun around to the back of the class with the rest of the dancers, she caught Patrick looking at her; he was a beat too slow before he started his spin. His eyes appeared to be sad and lost this time. different than the emotionless look they had the other day. *That's too bad,* she thought to herself for a half second, and then pushed the intrusive thought out of her body and finished the routine. Before she knew it, practice was done for the day, and everyone around her was giving her props and letting her know how impressed they were. "Thank you!" Amelia repeated several times to each person who complimented her. "Have you been secretly recording our routines and practicing the entire time you were away?" Charisse joked. "I wish! I just picked up what I could while I was observing and practiced a little bit last night after the kids went to bed," Amelia responded. "Kudos to you. You're all caught up now. We have a new dance we are learning tomorrow for the end of the show," said Charisse. "I'm ready for it," Amelia replied.

Frederick and Dylan ambushed Amelia as she was leaving the studio. "We have some unfinished business to take care of," Frederick said in a serious tone. "What are you, mafia?" Amelia asked sarcastically. "Please hear him out, I can be the moderator, if need be," said Dylan, "We'll meet at my place right now," Frederick suggested. "No way, I have to feed my cat and walk my dog," Amelia responded.

"I'll help with that," Dylan offered. "I can't let you do that. Why would you want to do that?" Amelia asked. "Because I really care about this guy right here, and he really cares about you," Dylan said, while pointing at Frederick. "You'll never get past my door man," Amelia responded. "I can charm my way through any door," Dylan insisted. "Fine, if you insist, I'll text you the instructions," said Amelia.

Dylan headed east to Amelia's apartment, while Amelia and Frederick headed west to Frederick's apartment. "You have a really good friend there," Amelia said as they entered Frederick's apartment. "I sure do. In fact, I am hoping it's more than that," Frederick admitted. "Frederick, do you actually have feelings for someone? I think hell might freeze over," Amelia joked. "Do *you* have feelings for someone, missy?" Frederick asked. "I don't know to whom you are referring," said Amelia, acting shy. "Enough beating around the bush. This is about Patrick. And I hate being put in the middle," Frederick said loudly. The pitch of his voice must've startled his cat because the cat jumped into Amelia's lap. "I don't care if I never speak to Patrick again," she said. Her face was cold and resigned, but the subtle quiver of her lips told another story.

Amelia ignored Frederick and started petting the cat. "On another know, we are both cat owners now, how cute!" said Frederick. "You're right. It is about Patrick. And you shouldn't be in the middle. I am like a sister to you and Patrick is as good as a stranger," Amelia argued. "You, me, Patrick and Dylan are a foursome of besties now," responded Frederick. "No, we are not. Patrick has Veronica now. And you knew it. You knew it and didn't tell me. I had to find out at a late-night coffee shop," Amelia said with sadness in her voice. Next, the cat jumped out of Amelia's lap and dove into Frederick's lap headfirst. "Thanks for jumping ship and then returning," Frederick commented to his cat, and got purred at in return.

"Don't write me off so quickly. You never gave me a chance to explain. Patrick felt abandoned when you left and cut off contact. I had no idea what was going on because you cut me off as well in case you forgot," Frederick explained. "Blame the victim. Sounds about right," Amelia interjected. "If you'll allow me to continue," Patrick struck back. "Please do," Amelia replied. "Dylan and I comforted Patrick. We were all also busy with the rehearsals, but he did the best we could to remind him how much you cared about him and would be coming back. The next thing I know, Veronica showed up in town right before you were scheduled to arrive. She's a stage five clinger and I haven't had the chance to talk to him. I tried to hear him out the day before rehearsals, since I knew it would be your first rehearsal back, but ended up giving him hell, hence the pensive looks on our faces. I still don't know the full story, but I know you deserve to know," Frederick stated. "What more is there to know? She's still in town hanging out with him. The writing is on the wall," said Amelia. "I know he loves you. I see it on his face. Give him a chance to explain. At least tell him how you really feel," said Frederick.

"Why don't you tell Dylan how you really feel?" asked Amelia. "I think that's obvious, I'm not as adept at hiding my emotions as you are," Frederick responded. "You need to say the words. Words are important," said Amelia. "I will if you will," said Frederick. "Are we really doing this again?" Amelia asked. "Yes!" said Frederick. What am I supposed to say?" asked Amelia vulnerably. "Just tell him how you feel. It's as simple as that," Frederick explained. "Simple is hard," Amelia claimed. "So is being lonely forever because you never spoke up," Frederick fired back.

While she was taking in his advice, Amelia looked on the wall of Frederick's living room and saw a frame with a poem in it that she had never seen before. It was a poem by Shel Silverstein that read: "She had blue skin, and so did he. He kept it hid and so did she. They searched for blue their whole life through, then passed right by- and never knew."

"When did you add that poem to your wall?" Amelia asked, changing the subject. "Recently. It's the background of Dylan's laptop and it spoke to me, so I had it made up and framed," Frederick responded. "You liked something, so you had it framed? Definitely not the words of a struggling twenty something year old dancer living in the big city," Amelia teased. "Our parents gave us something better than love, honesty and comfort; they gave us money," Frederick said without a glimpse of a smirk on his face to indicate that he was joking. "Oh, what am I going to do with you?" Amelia said as she smiled bigly. "I don't know but you're stuck with me forever, and maybe Dylan too now," Frederick said, and initiated one of their iconic twenty second hugs; the kitten snoke his way into the hug as well.

Before she knew it, Amelia was on her way home, and their friendship was restored. Her phone started buzzing and she assumed it was Frederick being needy, but the number that popped up on her screen was "Heidi." She had almost forgotten about the two lovely ladies she met on the golf course. "Hello, how are you?" Amelia said when she picked up the phone call. "Doing well, I'm in town and thought I'd give you a ring so we can discuss my favor to you that I promised when I got back in town," Heidi said in an official, professional tone. It had slipped Amelia's mind that she had enlisted a stranger to find her mother, and that her mother was in New York City, allegedly. Her mind was spinning in a million different directions. She felt like she was in a game at Sports Plus where you had to whack each alligator that popped up within seconds or you'd lose. "What was it called? Oh, right, alligator whack-a-mole!" Amelia was thinking but must've verbalized half of the thought aloud as Heidi shouted, "What in the name of god are you talking about?" on the other end of the phone. "I said I have to catch you later," Amelia said, trying to save herself from the embarrassing slip of the tongue.

"Let's grab dinner tomorrow," Heidi invited Amelia, instead of agreeing to catch up later. She never backed down and wasn't about to start. She was determined to help someone and to that extent, make her life meaningful. There was a selfish component of the "favor" for Heidi. Amelia suspected it and was happy to somehow return the favor. "You tell me where," said Amelia. "Do you ever venture to the Upper East Side?" Heidi asked. "I didn't pin you as the uptight Upper East type," Amelia commented. "Of course I am, I'm old, and that's where all my best clients were. All the ones who wanted their husbands investigated. I made bank. There were no hip downtown places to live back in my day," Heidi responded. "Those are all good points. I would love to make my way over there, it'll take me almost an hour, though, with the tourist traffic," Amelia explained. "No rush, I have all the time in the world. Can you meet me at Water & Wheat?" suggested Heidi. "Sounds trendy enough for me," Amelia said with tongue and cheek. "See you there, let me know when you are on your way," said Hedi, and the call ended.

When Amelia made the last turn onto her block, she noticed a handsome Irish Bostonian guy arguing with her doorman.

Her heart started beating out of her chest. Neither of the men noticed her since they were enthralled in their verbal altercation. It wasn't like Patrick, what she knew of him, to be short with service workers, and that was curious to Amelia. She was also impressed at her doorman for not allowing anyone to get passed, especially a man he hadn't recognized. "He's getting an extra generous tip this Christmas," Amelia said to herself. New York was one of the only perfectly acceptable places to talk to yourself out loud and no one around you will think twice. Amelia took advantage of this opportunity to process all the happenings in her life as of late.

As she got closer to the front entrance of her building, the scene of the crime, Amelia overheard the two men speaking in frustrated tones. "Please let me in. I need to see her," Patrick pleaded. "Sir, you are not on Ms. Chaplan's guest list, and I do not recognize you as a frequent visitor. It is against the rules," said the doorman. "Forget the rules. This is important. I need to see her," Patrick repeated. "I can't allow that. This is a fully secured building, and you are a stranger. Please stop making a scene and leave the premises at once," the doorman said in a stern voice. "That won't be necessary,"

Amelia said, and both of the men became startled at the sound of her soft voice. "My apologies, Ms. Chaplan. I didn't see his name on the list," the doorman apologized. "No, I'm sorry, I should have told you I was coming," Patrick interjected. "No need for anyone to apologize. This seems like an honest misunderstanding. Patrick, we can talk in the common area on the first floor. Follow me," said Amelia.

"Once again, let me start for apologizing for intruding like this," Patrick began to say. "You know my dad once told me it's better to not do anything to be sorry about in the first place," Amelia interrupted. "I can explain," Patrick chimed in. "I don't think an explanation is warranted. It was pretty clear what's going on at the coffee shop the other night. Finding out in front of Charisse was the cherry topping on an awful week," said Amelia. "Veronica just left and went back to Massachusetts," Patrick stated. "Why? And why would I care?" Amelia responded to the statement in question form. "I think Veronica being here was a blessing in disguise for you. It obviated the need for you to confront how you feel about me and take a chance," Patrick surmised. "Oh yes, what a blessing, however should I repay you both?" Amelia said mockingly. For the next few minutes, they went back and forth like children, avoiding talking about their feelings, and mocking each other. Luckily, they were interrupted by Amelia's doorman, which stopped the immature banter from going on indefinitely. They were like two children poking each other on the playground, adding insult to injury.

"Excuse me!" the doorman shouted, and their voices instantaneously went silent, as if they were getting in trouble by their teacher. Speaker of teachers, Professor Bryant was standing alongside the doorman. "Miss, you have another visitor. I didn't recognize him this man either, but you seem to be letting anyone in these days," the doorman said sassily. "I think that's my cue to leave," said Patrick, and he scurried out the door as the doorman held it open, never one to be distracted from his job duties, ever the professional.

"Professor Bryant, what on earth are you doing in my building! We are on school break!" Amelia shouted, carrying the same energy from her conversation with Patrick. "I didn't mean to disturb you, Ms. Chaplan. I got your address from the Christmas card you sent me with the picture of you and your dog, the one I helped rescue," Professor Bryant explained. "I do recall. You are always welcome,

Professor, I'm just taken back. I haven't seen you since the semester ended. It's not every day you run into your professor in your lobby during winter break," said Amelia, softening up her stance. She felt stupid and rude for her initial dramatic reaction to his presence. "I see that you're signed up for one of my classes for the upcoming Spring semester, so you're not getting away from me that easily," said Professor Bryant. "You make a good point. I signed up for those classes way in advance. That can always be changed," said Amelia with her eyebrows furrowed, hands on her hips, fingers pointing, and with half a smile on her face.

Professor Bryant started stuttering and mumbled something. After a few seconds, actual words started coming out of his mouth. "Fair enough. The real reason I am here is to talk about Charisse. We've had a whirlwind romance, all thanks to you. You are our only mutual connection. That's the only reason I am coming to you. As crazy as this sounds, I would like to propose to her on New Year's Eve, after the show, of course. I need to know if she has any family that I can consult before the proposal. Has she talked to you about family at all? Anything you know would be helpful. I'm an old school guy. She's never talked about her family to me, but I absolutely don't want to leave them out of it. I want to plan a little surprise party for her. This is true love at first sight, and I am the happiest I've ever been. Wow, that was a lot to get off my chest," said Professor Bryant in a long-winded explanation of why he was in his former student's lobby at night.

"It's okay to breathe. Let me digest this for a moment. You want to propose to my choreographer who you met during a random karaoke night?" Amelia asked in astonishment. "When you say it like that, it does sound crazy," Professor Bryant admitted. "Crazy? Crazy doesn't even begin to describe it. I've seen her several times since then and she hasn't mentioned you at all," Amelia blurted out. "Gee thanks, now I feel a lot better about asking her to spend the rest of her life with me," Professor Bryant replied. "No, no, I didn't mean it like that. You weren't kidding when you said the truth is stranger than fiction," said Amelia. "Agreed," replied Professor Bryant. Amelia thought for a moment while they stood there in silence. "You know, she hasn't mentioned family to me, but I just may have an idea crazier than yours. I met a private investigator out in Arizona," said Amelia; a wild idea popped into her head concurrently as she spoke, and she didn't have time to wonder if she might later regret the offer. "Say more!" Professor Bryant said eagerly.

"If you insist. I went home to Arizona after being notified that I had a phenomenal offer on my family home only to find out that my mother is not my biological mother, played a round of golf with my family estate attorney, and met a private investigator who lives in New York City and is going to find my mother. I'm meeting with her tomorrow for dinner and can ask her if she can find the information about Charisse's family that you are seeking," Amelia explained. "Wow, the truth is indeed stranger than fiction," Professor Bryant noted. "This might sound crazy, but I'd pay her handsomely if she can find Charisse's family," he added. "For some reason I don't think money is her motivation, but I think she'd love to help," said Amelia. "And you think this based on a round of golf you played with her?" Professor Bryant asked skeptically. "Yes," Amelia said matter of factly. "Well then, keep me in the loop," Professor Bryant said before he left the building. The doorman shook his head in disapproval.

You're not having an affair with your professor, are you?" the doorman asked Amelia the next morning as she was heading out the door. "God no, where are your manners?" Amelia asked. "I am paid to protect this building, and that little lover's quarrel last night was quite the scene. Additionally, I need to know what to tell the other guests who come to see you," he responded in the most professional tone possible. "There will be no more guests! Don't let anyone in!" Amelia yelled as she hurried out of the building before any of her neighbors overhead. It was New York City though, who actually knew their own neighbors?

Chapter 22: Heidi

Heidi arrived at her humble abode townhouse on the Upper East Side. It had been in her family for decades, too old and outdated to sell for its true value, so it would remain forever in the family until someone appreciated it enough to make a decent offer. The new millennial young professionals pouring into the city made downtown a more desirable place to leave than the stuffy Upper East Side. Finally, people were coming to their senses, was what Heidi told everyone. She was never one to cozy up to high society, but she also couldn't turn down the opportunities her family presented her with. Being a law enforcement officer or private investigator, she couldn't pay the bills in a place within the city more than 200 square feet. This is precisely why Amelia's case spoke to her. Growing up with wealthy parents in a country club-like setting, and managing to grow into a normal, down-to-earth young adult was rare, and she reminded Heidi of herself when she was twenty-something year old.

It was more than retirement that motivated Heidi to want more of a purpose in life. She had always been searching for meaning beyond financial stability, given that she always had that. She thought about Amelia's case for the entirety of the plane ride from Arizona to New York. The first thing she did as soon as she got home was to call Amelia and set up a dinner to discuss the case so she could start officially working on it and making a miracle happen.

Heidi left her townhouse for the first time that day to meet Amelia for dinner. She only had to walk two blocks to the trendy restaurant that she had assumed catered to millennials like her.

Heidi walked right up to Amelia and hugged her when she recognized her from the golf course. Heidi also showed up to engagement fifteen minutes earlier to scope things out, but Amelia seemingly beat her to the punch, even though she had a much longer walk through the cold. It was the one day in December that it hadn't snowed, a record-breaking winter for the books, in the big city.

"It's nice to see you on the other side," Amelia greeted Heidi after receiving the hug. "It's nice to see you made it here to the upper side. Did you need to show your passport?" Heidi asked. "I forgot my passport, but they let me through midtown," Amelia responded in jest.

"Seriously, I'm glad you made it back home safely. I know we have some work to do. Let's get down to business," said Heidi. "Sure, let's not waste time. Just the type of private investigator I want, straightforward," Amelia responded. "I've put a lot of thought into your case on the plane, where I do my best thinking," said Heidi. "That's great, but I don't have much information to give you. I didn't have much family beyond my parents and all I have is this letter from my mother with sparce details," Amelia said as she handed the envelope to Heidi. "I'll take good care of this letter and return it when I'm done, but I'd like to have it handy to reflect on it and come up with ideas," Heidi stated. "I think that's a fine idea," Amelia agreed.

"I do have another proposition," said Amelia timidly. "I love a good proposition, I think," said Heidi hesitantly. "I have a friend who also needs help tracking down the family of the woman he is hoping to propose marriage to. He wants to know if you can help. I know, it sounds outlandish, right?" said Amelia. "It does, and I can," said Heidi agreeably. "Are you sure? He wants to propose by New Year's Day, so you won't have much time," Amelia warned. "I've met deadlines quicker than that. All I can do is my best. Now, do you have a deadline for your case?" Heidi inquired. "I've been waiting my whole life, and I didn't know it, so I think I can wait a little bit longer. Plus, I don't want to get my hopes up," Amelia stated. "It would be unkind not to tell you that things may not work out the way you expected, so you should have no hopes or expectations going into this," said Heidi. "Understood. I am completely realistic about getting a happy ending in all of this," Amelia responded. "And I am not paid to provide happy endings, only answers," Heidi added. "You're being clear. And I would just like an ending to this madness as well as answers once and for all," said Amelia. "Right, you're my favorite type of client," said Heidi. Their conversation was interrupted by their young, hipster, waitress who was eager to list the specials and all their special cocktails, none of which Heidi was interested in. She was a glass of scotch neat type of woman truth be told, but she politely listened with Amelia. They spent the rest of the dinner talking golf.

At the end of dinner, Amelia gifted Heidi a Ben Hogan golf book that she had been using to improve her swing ever since she returned from Arizona. She'd stay up reading until Ballare and Coro fell asleep. Since Heidi refused to accept payment for her services, it was the least Amelia could do. It was a kind, thoughtful gesture, and Heidi expressed her appreciation for it immensely by thanking her profusely. Amelia's dad taught her at a young age that it was the little things that made the biggest difference.

Heidi walked back to her upper east side digs that evening with a renewed sense of purpose. Not one but two people were relying on her to somehow change their lives. She was beyond confident that she was up for the tasks. She slept peacefully that night, woke up to the sound of roosters on the rooftop animal hospital on the corner, and the first phone call she made was to her former assistant, Patty, letting her know she'd need her help. Patty was also retired and living in Queens; a hop, skip and jump away from the upper east side.

Heidi stayed up until two in the morning shooting off emails to gather additional information. The adrenaline rush did not allow her body to sleep without working. Amelia had provided her with Professor Bryant's email address to contact him if needed. When Heidi got a case, she jumped right into it and gave it her all from the start. She even became borderline obsessed. Since taking a break to golf around the country, Amelia's case was her first and she was more than thrilled to work on two at once.

Chapter 23: The Meet-up

Patrick went straight to bed that evening after dance rehearsal. He was repeatedly awoken by his phone buzzing nonstop. He opened his phone and saw the name "Veronica" appear with 50 missed calls and dozens of unread text messages. He told her two days ago that he was in love with Amelia, they would not be getting back together and insisted that she go back home to Massachusetts and move on with her life. Veronica wasn't one to take no for an answer, and she wasn't used to being turned down, that was for sure. Patrick was less sympathetic towards her after she nearly destroyed his chances with Amelia, his true love, who may never know how he felt.

The text messages and voicemails from Veronica poured in throughout the evening and late at night. She begged for his mercy, apologizing, pleading, and sought clarification. She told him what a great time they were having during her visit to New York, meanwhile the entire time he was trying to come up with an excuse to make her leave. She brought up their encounter with Amelia and Charisse at the coffee shop. Veronica expressed that she knew he had feelings for

Amelia the second they ran into her, and she concluded that Amelia was the reason he essentially sent Veronica packing. It was all true. Patrick couldn't even bother to muster up the energy to make up a lie or denial.

Patrick tossed and turned, checked his phone, and debated blocking Veronica. He didn't block her out of fear that she may randomly show up in person again and surprise him in New York. Every time he checked his phone, he secretly hoped it was Amelia reaching out to him, and he was let down each time he realized it was still Veronica begging him back.

After hours of avoidance, and at his wits end, Patrick finally handed his phone on the hundredth ring. "Veronica, I want nothing to do with you! I'm in love with someone else!" he shouted into the phone and hung up before she could respond. Then, he went into his phone settings and blocked Veronica out of his life literally and figuratively. Patrick called his mother, Kelly, and told her everything that happened in the past few days with Veronica and Amelia. He had no one else to turn to and he desperately needed some old school "mom" advice, as much as he hated to admit it.

"You did the right thing, sweetheart. I never liked Veronica. She always thought she was too good for you, which couldn't be further from the truth. And to show up in New York like that without any notice? The nerve of her! She could've ruined things for you and Amelia," Kelly complained. "I think she did, mom. Amelia won't talk to me; she barely looks at me during rehearsals. I messed up big time. I don't know if we could come back from this," Patrick lamented. "Don't beat yourself up over it. You did nothing wrong. This is all Veronica's fault," Kelly echoed the sentiment. "Mom, what do I do? I've gotten myself into a real pickle this time, and real feelings are there," said Patrick. "My son asking me for help is like music to my ears. I'd love to solve this situation for you. However, when it comes to love, it's best you figure it out yourself," Kelly responded. "I will be there front and center to watch your show on New Year's Eve," she added. "You're coming in person? You know it's being televised nationally, and you can watch it from the comfort of your home in Boston," said Patrick. "I wouldn't miss it for the world. My oldest best friend and my son in the same show in the most exciting city on the planet!" Kelly exclaimed. "Well, if you put it that way," Patrick replied. "I'm not going to tell you exactly what to do, but I suggest whatever you do includes telling Amelia how you feel before New Year's Day," Kelly recommended. "I'll take that under advisement," Patrick responded sarcastically. "Ha, ha, ha," Kelly replied before she ended the phone call and left Patrick to his own devices.

Patrick typed and deleted several messages to Amelia, now that Veronica was no longer blowing up his phone. After much contemplating, he settled on: *Can we talk?* He hesitated for a few seconds and then sent the text message. The message turned green, and a red exclamation point showed that the message wasn't sent. *I blocked Veronica and Amelia blocked me, that's karma for you,* he thought to himself. "I'll have to think of some other way to get through to Amelia, and I don't have much time," Patrick said to himself.

"I need your help," Patrick said as soon as Frederick answered his phone call. "And you're asking me why?" Patrick said rudely. "Because you're the one person who can get through to Amelia and she values your opinion. I need your approval," Patrick pleaded. "I do not approve of men who lead my sweetheart friend on and then go back with an ex the second she leaves town," Frederick shouted into the phone. "I would like to have the opportunity to explain it to you, and this time to have a more civil meet up. I care about Amelia, and I don't want to lose her for good," Patrick begged. "Why should I trust you?" Frederick asked, indicating that he was warming up to the idea of a second meeting with Patrick. Patrick let out a sigh of relief that Frederick was giving him a chance to explain himself and answer questions; he'd take anything he could get at this point.

"I think I'm in love with her," Patrick stated. "You think?" Frederick pushed him to be more decisive. "No, I know. I am in love with your best friend, Amelia. There, I said it," Patrick revealed. "Patrick! I think a single tear is coming down my cheek. I agree to meet up with you, but only if Dylan can come too," Frederick replied emotionally. "I will meet up with you ONLY if Dylan can come," Patrick agreed. "I'll send you the place and time. We'll meet tomorrow after rehearsals," Patrick said and then hung up the phone.

The next day at rehearsal was the new status quo. Frederick and Dylan were attached at the hip, while Amelia and Patrick kept their distance at opposite ends of the studio. Professor Bryant stood at the doorway at the end of class to walk Charisse home, some days waiting with flowers in his hands. It was old school romance you didn't come across in the city anymore. Charisse tried to play it off like it was no big deal, but all the dancers could see beyond her words, especially Patrick. He wished that he could express his love for Amelia so easily and flawlessly as Professor Bryant did for Charisse.

After rehearsal, Patrick met up with Frederick and Dylan, ironically at the same late night coffee shop that he had the run in with Veronica, Amelia and Charisse. It was the most convenient, quietest location, and they were unlikely to run into Amelia. She probably swore off that place forever the night of their run in, Patrick surmised. Frederick agreed with this position, and Dylan went along with it as he did any of Frederick's crazy ideas, as long as they didn't involve alcohol. "Thank you, guys, for meeting me here," Patrick greeted them. "You're buying our coffees," Frederick responded. "Frederick, let's be nice, no demands," Dylan intervened, as was his job. "I am more than happy to buy the coffees. Everything is on me tonight," Patrick stated. "That's very generous," said Dylan. They each ordered and then found a secluded table in the back of the room to talk in private.

Patrick felt his skin flushing before he began to speak, "Let me be Frank. I want nothing to do with Veronica. I am completely done with her. Her visit was unwelcome, and I told her as much right before I blocked all communication from her. I am in love with Amelia," Patrick explained. "Do you promise?" Frederick asked firmly in a rough voice. "How about simply bringing her flowers?" Dylan chimed in. "Dear god no, Dylan. Flowers are already dead. That's the biggest waste of money," Frederick fumed. "I wasn't aware that you were cognizant of money spending and savings," Dylan responded. "Without frugality none can be rich, and with it very few would be poor," Frederick quoted his favorite thinker. "You continue to pleasantly surprise me," Dylan complimented him as a puppy looks at its new owner. "Guys, sorry to break up the sentimental moment and all, but I don't have much time here," Patrick interjected, while shuffling his feet.

"Sorry," Dylan immediately apologized after his momentary admiration for Frederick was interrupted, which left him nonplussed, and he quickly adjusted his mind back to reality as he was conditioned to do throughout his childhood years. On the other hand, Frederick was completely unfazed by Patrick's interruption and wanted to relish the moment that he noticed his crush falling for him.

"It's fine. Now what am I going to do to win Amelia back?" Patrick asked. "Something that doesn't include a bouquet of already dead flowers," Frederick added. "I have an idea. A good friend of mine proposed to his then fiancé on Boston Harbor under the fireworks at the stroke of midnight on New Year's Day. Suffice to say it turned out well and they are now happily married. Can we extrapolate that and make it happen in New York City on the East River?" Dylan asked. "I'm not proposing! She will barely even speak to me. I just want to profess my love," Patrick protested. "Although that's a good suggestion for Professor Bryant. I hear through the grapevine that he is going to propose to Charisse, and there will be fireworks at the end of our show," Frederick blurted out. "What?!" Patrick and Dylan shouted in disbelief. Frederick eyes grew too big for his face, and the look of regret overcame him. "I suppose I wasn't supposed to say anything," he said, with his fingers grabbing his lower mouth.

"Way to keep a secret! How can I trust that you'll keep this whole thing under wraps?" Patrick yelled. "I guess you have no choice now, do you?" Frederick yelled back. "Break it up, boys, we are veering off course," Dylan yelled at both of them. "Professor Bryant is going to steel my thunder; I wanted to do something grand," Patrick complained. "Maybe we should tell him so we can coordinate?" Frederick asked. "No!" Dylan and Patrick screamed at him.

"Do we know what company handles the fireworks above the East River on New Year's Day at midnight?" Patrick asked reluctantly. "Um, no?" Dylan responded. "I may know a guy," Frederick replied. "You can't be serious. I was being facetious with the question," Patrick said. "Apparently, he's kind of a big deal in the big city," Dylan teased. "Kind of a big deal? I AM a big deal! And my father owes me a favor anyway. He may have some connections in the mayor's office," Frederick said nonchalantly as if having a powerful father was no big deal. "If you can pull this off, I'd owe you a blank check for life, man," Patrick said enthusiastically. "I don't accept blank checks. And I don't write them. As long as you keep Amelia happy, you'll never owe me anything," Frederick reassured him.

"What exactly are we doing with the fireworks?" Dylan asked.

"Something just came to mind, but I don't want to say it until I know for sure if Frederick can pull strings," said Patrick. Kelly was always a little superstitious, and Patrick inherited that trait. He didn't like to say things he wanted aloud to the universe should his plans not come to fruition; it was bad luck in his opinion. "I'll reach out to my father and get back to you," Frederick promised. They finished their coffees and their meeting came to an end as they parted ways.

Frederick called his father on the walk back to his apartment. It was a conversation that he was avoiding, but needed to be had, and this was a perfect excuse. He hadn't returned his father's phone calls since he ran into him at the restaurant with the dancing crew. *Sometimes the best way to get over things is to go through them,* Frederick thought to himself before he dialed his father's phone number. His father answered on the first ring, a stark contrast to his childhood when he never picked up. "Freddy?" he said in a surprised tone. "If you call me Freddy again, I am hanging up," Frederick replied sternly. "Got it," said his father. "If I may, I have a favor to ask of you," Frederick said. "Anything you want," his father immediately replied. *This reminds me of Cat in the Cradle by Harry Chapin,* Frederick thought to himself. His father went from being a cutthroat businessman and absentee father, to a bumbling beggar in a matter of a few years. Frederick felt sort of bad for his father in that moment, and he grasped the phone tighter to his ear and took it off speakerphone as if he wanted to absorb his new father's words into his ear.

"Do you need some money, or a job at the company?" Frederick's father asked. "No dad, I do not want money, and I do not want a job. Between the trust fund and dancing I am doing quite well. I'm also still in college if you have forgotten," Frederick responded. "Fair enough, sorry," his father replied apologetically. "And you are not going to get anything in return. This is not a quid pro quo situation. It's a father helping his son," Frederick clarified. "Understood," his father said, towing the line so as not to say anything too much that could be scrutinized. "I have a special request from a dear friend of mine regarding the fireworks that are handled by the mayor's office on New Year's Eve," Frederick said. "What in the world does your friend have to do with the fireworks?" his dad asked in shock. "No questions, no judgement, just results," Frederick quipped back. "I'll see what I can do. The mayor does have a blank check written out to me," he responded. "Of course you do, dad. I don't have specifics yet, but I just need if we can arrange something with the fireworks," Frederick reiterated. There was a moment of silence.

"Are you there?" Frederick asked. "Yes, it was just really nice to hear you call me dad. You've been calling me by my first name your whole life," his father said. "Yeah, yeah," Frederick responded. "Yes, I do have undue influence on the mayor's fireworks show. You have my word," his dad responded. "You better stick to your word this time," Frederick warned. "Absolutely," his father swiftly responded.

"And one more thing, son," Patrick's father added. "Yes?" Patrick responded inquisitively. "Promise me a father on New Year's Day brunch, like the old times," Frederick's father humbly requested. "You mean that one time, a long time ago?" Frederick clarified. "Well, yes," his father answered. "I think I could make it. Could you make it to my show on New Year's Eve?" Frederick asked, astounded that the question escaped his lips. Frederick's grip on the phone loosened finally, he rested the phone on his living room coffee table and held his ear in pain. The part of his ear that he held the phone up to was red and as sore as a childhood ear infection.

Frederick rubbed his ear and then gleefully called Patrick to inform him of the good news. "Thank you so much, man," said Patrick. "So, tell me what your plan is," Frederick said. "I wanted to get something special in the sky for Amelia. Some kind of fireworks or lights among the fireworks with her name," Patrick stated. "Hmm, you are on the right track, yet something original might be more fitting," Frederick commented. "Do you have any ideas?" Patrick asked. "Let me give it a think for a while. I know we don't have much time. We also need to give my dad's people time to prepare it, so how about we take a couple days and then execute the plan we come up with, all while perfecting our dance routine?" Frederick asked. "If there ever were a place to get this done, it would certainly be New York," Patrick responded. "Only in New York," Patrick reiterated.

Chapter 24: The Proposal Plan

The day after Amelia met with Heidi after dance rehearsal, she met with Professor Bryant. The meeting was planned in advance this time. She had reached out to Professor Bryant not only to relay the information from Heidi, but to offer help in planning the proposal for Charisse.

Due to pure exhaustion, mentally and physically, Amelia didn't have the wherewithal to think of anywhere else to meet her former professor than Mocha Lattes. The last couple weeks left her bereft of brain power. He didn't have any better ideas of where to meet anyway. She gave the professor an energized hug, despite feeling sluggish, the second she saw him. Something about the sweetness of the situation won over her mostly cynical heart. He did need some help in the romance planning department, and Amelia felt an urge to provide that for him. It was a very rewarding volunteer project for her, and it didn't hurt that it took her mind off Patrick and her mother after dance rehearsals.

Charisse reassured Amelia throughout the past few days that she was caught up with the dance routines and would do fine in the show. She was blown away by Charisse' kindness; it was a rarity in a city where people bump your shoulder walking by without so much as a grin nor eye contact. She wanted to help Charisse have the most romantic proposal in the city that money can't buy.

"I got that," Professor Bryant said as he handed the barista a fistful of cash. "You don't have to pay for my tea," Amelia said. "It's the least I could do," he insisted, and Amelia agreed to let him pay so they wouldn't hold up the line of impatient people trying to get a coffee on their way home from work as fast as possible. Amelia waited for her tea and then they found a table at the back of the café.

"First, thank you so much for meeting me today, especially after the kerfuffle in your lobby. I have been trying to think of romantic ideas for days, I am bereft of brain power," Professor Bryant explained. He looked nervous, which seemed to be par for the course lately, and he was rubbing the top of his legs, something he did when he was in social situations outside of class, Amelia observed. Amelia noticed that Professor Bryant acted differently in front of Charisse. *I guess that's what true love does to a man, not that I would know,* Amelia thought to herself. The thought of a well-respected professor at a prestigious college in the city getting tongue-tied in front of a woman he cared about, melted her heart like an ice cream on a hot summer day. She was in awe of her professor, and the kind way he held Charisse in such a high regard after just knowing her a few weeks.

"Have you considered keeping it simple? The simplest answer is often the correct one. And then of course we will add personal romantic touches," Amelia suggested. "You're in the wrong field; you should be an engagement consultant," Professor Bryant joked. The corny, dumb jokes were part of his endearment, and Amelia faked laughter to be kind. "Are you incorporating your family at all?" Amelia inquired. "I don't have any family. My wife was my only family, and now I have none," Professor Bryant answered. Amelia didn't press any further. She knew the pain of having to answer questions about family all too well. *The lack of family seems to be a theme in this city,* Amelia thought to herself. "Speaking of family, have you heard from Heidi?" Amelia asked. "I have been emailing back and forth with her thee past couple days, but so far, no updates.

Have you heard any exciting news about your case?" he asked gently, being careful not to pry too much. "Crickets. Nothing new. Not getting my hopes up," Amelia responded dryly. "It could take months or years," Professor Bryant added. "But you'll go through with the proposal on New Year's Eve either way, correct?" asked Amelia. "Oh yes, I can barely wait," said Professor Bryant. "What are some things Charisse loves that I wouldn't know about?" Professor Bryant asked. "Green tea, flowers. But I'm sure you already know that. You know, on second thought, she seems understated, but I'd bet all women appreciate pomp and circumstance when it comes to romance," Amelia stated, processing her thoughts aloud. "What about one of those helicopters that fly over the beach with a banner attached to it?" Professor Bryant suggested. "That would be nice except it's going to be dark out and won't be able to see the sign," Amelia noted. "Good point," he responded. Probably a cheesy idea anyway," Professor Bryant stated. "Not as cheesy as a baseball game proposal," Amelia replied. "What about a dinner boat ride across the East River under the midnight fireworks?" Professor Bryant asked. "It'll be too cold. I don't think they do dinner cruises in the dead of winter, and if they did,

Charisse is an Arizona girl at heart, remember," Amelia responded.

"You know, an idea just popped into my head now that you mentioned the East River. Charisse once told me she originally grew up near Salt River, a part of Arizona that was known for having wild horses, and I know she loves animals. Why not incorporate horses?" Amelia asked. "Like a romantic, old school, horse carriage ride around Central Park?" Professor Bryant replied. "Now you're talking," said Amelia. "Is too cliché?" Professor Bryant asked with trepidation. "It's not cliché, it's classic," Amelia corrected him. "Do the Central Park carriage rides even go until midnight?" Professor Bryant asked. "How am I going to get a horse drawn carriage through the streets of Manhattan at the stroke of midnight on New Year's Eve?" Professor Bryant asked sarcastically. "I may know someone," Amelia said matter of factly. "Just like you knew someone who could find Charisse's family. How do you know someone in this city for everything? And the random trips out of town? Are you CIA? How many fixers do you know?" Professor Bryant asked suspiciously with paranoia in his tone. "Just the two," Amelia responded humorously.

"Are you a spy? Who sent you? I guess the CIA didn't like my thesis on the negative mental health impact the agency has on their rank-and-file employees. Is Charisse a spy?" Professor Bryant said as he started to freak out.

"Okay, just calm down, we are in a public place. You are acting out of pocket because you are in love and nervous about proposing. I'm pretty sure she's going to say yes. All we need to do is plan something romantic. I can speak to my friend Frederick about the horse drawn carriage. It might cost you a pretty penny, but I am certain he can help pull it off," Amelia said as she grabbed both of Professor Bryant's arms tightly to calm his body and looked him directly in the eye. It was a technique she learned, coincidently, in one of Professor Bryant's classes. *Sometimes it may be true, those who can't do, teach,* Amelia thought to herself as she was settling him down. *Writing a published paper on the negative effectives of the CIA, now that's badass,* Amelia also thought to herself. "So, you'll talk to your friends Frederick and Heidi?" Professor Bryant wanted to confirm with Amelia before parting ways. "I'll make some phone calls tonight.

Did you pick out a ring?" Amelia double checked. "The ring! Oh, my goodness, I may have overlooked that little detail," Professor Bryant answered. "That minor detail is what the entire proposal revolves around, professor. Why do men need so much help in the romance department?" Amelia asked rhetorically while shaking her head. Professor Bryant shrugged his shoulders and put his hands up in the air. "We are going to the diamond district. I hope you have cash. Do you need to stop at an ATM on the way?" Amelia said. "Will we pass a Chase bank?" Professor Bryant asked. "You mean the JP Morgan Chase bank that has a gold vault underneath that is connected to the New York Fed's gold vault? If that's what you mean then yes, we do pass one, and I'm quite sure there's an ATM you can access on the way," Amelia said confidently, having learned this information from Frederick, one of the many fun facts he had shared with her about the city.

"There goes my Christmas bonus," Professor Bryant said as he withdrew up to his daily limit at the JP Morgan Chase Bank ATM. "Maybe we should try to find the gold tunnel," he added. "Right now, we need to focus on finding a diamond," Amelia replied. I find the diamond industry to be unethical," Professor Bryant stated. "I beg your pardon?" said Amelia. "Should I mention the human rights abuses, water pollution, habitat destruction? Shall I continue? As a matter of fact, the lab-grown diamond industry is on the rise," Professor Bryant responded emphatically. "Professor Bryant! Human rights and environmental issues aside, every woman wants to be presented with a diamond when the man of their dreams gets on their knees and declares their undying love, even Charisse," Amelia strongly protested against his position. "I suppose there is not enough time to go searching for a lab grown diamond," Professor Bryant came to terms with his reality. "And the diamond district sure doesn't sell them," Amelia said. "It's not like you have to get a blood diamond. But you do have to leave there with something today, and you don't have too much room to negotiate," Amelia warned him. "Fair enough," Professor Bryant replied.

"Twenty grand is the lowest I'll go. This is a quality diamond," said the jeweler. "Then I'm walking to the next reseller. There's about fifty of you in this district. You need my business more than I need you. Amelia let's go!" said Professor Bryant sternly and loudly. *Who would've known the Professor had it in him? I guess you never really know someone until you see them do business, or at least that's what I've heard,* Amelia thought to herself.

"Fine, you got a deal, but only if you pay cash," the jeweler caved in to avoid losing a customer to the competition. "That's what I thought," Professor Bryant said confidently and then whipped out a wad of cash. It was if his alter ego had taken over the negotiations. He was nothing like the guy who was freaking out over Amelia knowing someone that could help with the horse-drawn carriage. *Interesting how certain situations draw out different parts of us,* Amelia observed quietly.

As the sky turned dark, Professor Bryant walked Amelia back to her apartment building, ring box in hand, holding the box for dear life. Amelia walked with a sense of pride that she had made a movie-like love story come true in real life and grateful that she got a front row seat to the happy ending.

When Amelia walked into her apartment, she was lovingly embraced by Ballare and Cora. She eagerly called Frederick, and he answered on the first ring. "Do you know someone who can arrange something for me on New Year's Eve?" she asked. "Why does someone always assume I know someone?" Frederick asked. "Because you know someone for everything," Amelia answered. "Don't give me platitudes. What do you need?" he asked. "I need a horse drawn carriage at midnight to assist with a proposal?" said Amelia bluntly. "For whom is this proposal for?" Frederick inquired. "Don't tell a soul if I tell you," Amelia made Frederick promise. "I promise," he said. "It's for Charisse," Amelia revealed. "Professor Bryant is proposing?" Frederick squealed in excitement. "Yes, and he wants to use one of those Central Park carriage ride horses," Amelia explained. "Of course, I know the guy who operates one of those. I'm his biggest tipper. Let me see what I can do," Frederick replied. "Frederick you are the best!" Amelia exclaimed. "Yeah, yeah, yeah. I know I am," responded Frederick. "Alright, thanks, love you, bye!" Amelia said to end the phone call.

Chapter 25: New Life Fertility Clinic

Heidi spent the past twenty-four hours on her computer researching Amelia's potential biological family. She completed a dozen background searches and family finder checks. She made hundreds of outgoing phone calls, *but who answers their phone calls for unknown numbers these days?* She murmured to herself in exasperation. On the other hand, it was much less perplexing to find Charisse's family for Professor Bryant. There was only one problem; her parents were deceased, and she had no siblings. There was no one for Professor Bryant to reach out to as far as Hiedi could tell. Luckily, some of her third and fourth cousins had signed up for Ancestry DNA, and she had a back channel to get this information. *Distant cousins are just not going to cut it. I barely knew my first cousins,* Heidi thought to herself.

Heidi may not have always used the most ethical means, but she towed the line when it came to the law for her clients. First, she phoned Jordana to pry for some confidential information, for the sake of their dear friend. "You heard her on the golf course, she needs my help. And I need your help. You're the only one who would be able to find out the name of the fertility clinic. I bet there's not too many in town. And I bet knowing Amelia's mother you can figure it out. I guarantee the mother left you a note too, and you found it too painful to tell Amelia about it," Heidi begged. She was bluffing, but she must've sounded convincing because Jordana coughed up the information like she was a prisoner being questioned in Guantanamo Bay. "Now, do your job, and find get Amelia's mother!" Jordana encouraged. "If I do, you are paying for our next round of golf," Heidi joked.

"There's no reason to let a tiny ethical violation stand in the way of me doing my job," Heidi said aloud while looking up the phone number to the clinic she found Amelia's parents used to find an egg donor. "New Life Fertility Clinic," Heidi said as she read the website heading. Speaking to herself out loud was how Heidi processed things in her brain, and it was a sign of higher intelligence, or so she liked to tell herself.

Heidi grabbed her phone and punched in the numbers on the contact page of the New Life Fertility Clinic website. "New Life

Fertility Clinic, how may I help you?" said a youthful, chipper, female voice on the other end side of the phone. "Hello, this is Dr. Andrews, I am calling to request medical records on one of my patients," Heidi responded. If she ever had to go under disguise as a doctor, she thought Dr. Andrews would be a professional name to go by. "What's the last name?" the female asked. Her tone changed from chipper to skittish. "Chaplan, shall I spell it?" Heidi asked, while perfectly maintaining her disguise. "We don't have anyone with that name in our system," the young lady replied, and she was clearly lying. "I think you do," Heidi responded. "Anyway, we don't give out medical records without a release with the patient's signature," she responded. Her tone changed once again, but this time from skittish to combative. Heidi knew it wouldn't be possible to get Mrs. Chaplan's signature at this point and she wouldn't cross the line to misdemeanor territory. So, she would try her last resort tactic: the threat.

"Listen here, little girl. You're going to go into your little computer system and find whatever records you have. You are then going to walk over to your fax machine and send me everything you have. If you do not comply with this request your boss, Dr. Daniel

Marker, will be sorry," Heidi threatened. A moment of silence followed. "What fax number should I send the records to?" she asked Heidi. "Boom!"

Heidi cheered after she received the fax. And that was that. Heidi learned over the years of working as a private detective that most people have things to hide, and things they rather not have come to the surface.

Moments later, Heidi heard a high-pitched beeping noise that indicated the fax machine was receiving an inbound fax. The machine was practically as old as her and sounded like a dying cat. A slew of paperwork arrived to Heidi via fax. The medical records, blood pressure numbers, etc. look completely forged with many cross outs and white out marks. Clearly, this clinic was not the type to take adequate medical records, but that was of no concern to Heidi to get her job done.

Heidi reviewed the intake paperwork. "Donor: Charisse Gardiner," Heidi read the first page aloud. "Why does that name sound so familiar," she asked herself. "Wait, how does this make sense? This can't be! What should I do? Who should I tell? First, I'll tell the Professor. No, first I'll tell Amelia. Ugh who knows anymore," Heidi contemplated aloud.

Heidi made a split-second decision and dialed Amelia. She sounded disoriented in response to the big news, and without the right words to express her emotions. It was a quick phone call. Next, Heidi called Professor Bryant. He seemed so elated to be proposing to Charisse the very next day that he didn't care about the lackluster news of her having no living family to share the moment with. He mentioned something about a horse and a diamond. Heidi glossed over the details, ended the phone call, shut her laptop and closed the cases.

Chapter 26: New Year's Eve

Everyone spent their Christmas holiday separately. Dylan flew home for one and a half days. Patrick took the train to Boston for the day. Frederick spent the day with his father. Amelia spent the day with her pets. Professor Bryant and Charisse had dinner together. The week between holidays went by in a flash.

It was New Year's Eve. Amelia was beside herself when Heidi delivered the news that Charisse Gardiner, her choreographer and friend, whose proposal she arranged, was her biological mother. "Charisse would've' had no way of knowing," Heidi reassured on the phone the night before. However, the New Year's Eve show was too important for Amelia to focus on anything else until after it was over, which was when Amelia planned on telling Charisse, sometime after Professor Bryant proposed. She hadn't had enough time to hammer out the details. "Guys, my performance is tonight, are you excited for mommy?" she asked Ballare and Coro. They just looked up at her, both at the same time, with the most innocent sets of eyes she had ever known, and then she squeezed them tightly in her arms. "I'll be home late tonight, guys. Your favorite doorman promised to come feed you and take you out for a walk at some point," Amelia told them. Amelia left her apartment that day, the last day of a wild year, with her head held high, ready to show the world what she had been practicing for most of her life. She headed uptown.

Over on the west side of the city, Frederick received a text message from his father on his way out of his building. "Everything is all set with the fireworks and horse. Break a leg tonight, kiddo," Frederick spoke as he read it. "At least he's trying," Frederick said, while shaking his head but also smiling. "Hold the fort down while I make two miracles happen tonight," he said to his cat and then shut the door behind him. Inspired by all the love and romance engulfing him, Frederick decided that tonight would be the night he officially told Dylan he loved him. It was long overdue, and so was his happiness.

As he walked from midtown, Patrick spoke to his mother, Kelly, on the phone. "The entire family is on the train. We'll be there in no time," she said. "You better sleep on the train. I can't wait for you guys to see what I have in store for Amelia at midnight," Patrick responded. "Patrick, you're killing me with anticipation! Anyway, good luck tonight!" Kelly said.

Dylan was making his way to the studio in a cab from the Upper West Side. He had woken up super early that morning to pick up his mother, father and sisters from the airport and just finished dropping them off at their hotel on the upper west side. This was the first time his father would see him in person following his passion and his stomach was full of butterflies.

Charisse said a little prayer at a church on the Upper East Side before heading south to the studio. It was a ritual she participated in before every one of her shows. Professor Bryant insisted on meeting her at a coffee shop on the Upper East Side and walking her. She found it a bit odd that he would want to meet her across the city just for a morning cup of tea but nevertheless agreed to it.

Professor Bryant thought it would quell his fears to see Charisse and spend time with her on the big day. He woke up an hour early to walk to the Upper East Side. Another calming technique he used was simply walking.

The clouds moved in, the temperature was in the twenties, but the snow held off, despite the forecast. The streets of the city were still white from the frequent December snowstorms that year. The dancers gathered in the studio and warmed up for hours before it was dress rehearsal time. Amelia kept her distance from Patrick; she still hadn't forgiven him. She kept her distance from Charisse and was awkward in their short interactions throughout the day. There was tension in the room palpable to everyone, videographers and production staff included. A behind-the-scenes documentary was being filmed for the show, something the dancers weren't informed of until that morning. "Are you sure everything is alright?" Charisse asked Amelia numerous times. "Doing fine, just the nerves getting to me a little bit," Amelia lied through her teeth.

Dylan kept Frederick on track each time he got distracted by texts from his father on his phone, finalizing arrangements for the evening. "Can you please focus? You just messed up your spin jump and it's not a good look to be on your phone while they're filming," Dylan chastised him. "I'll have my attorneys demand they remove the footage," Frederick responded. "Stop it, Frederick! You have an answer for everything! That's enough!" Dylan shouted as nearby dancers looked over in astonishment. "What is your problem, today?

"You're so uptight," Frederick whispered. Dylan took a deep breath. "Please forgive me. My dad being in town has made me a nervous wreck," said Dylan. "My dad is driving me nuts as well. I feel your pain. Let's try to be there for one another instead of using each other as punching bags," Frederick responded. "Agreed," Dylan said, and they hugged it out. A couple of the dancers around them clapped as a joke. Frederick did a curtsey and bowed in response.

"Time for hair and make-up, ladies and gentlemen!" Charisse announced. Please change into your costumes and get ready," she added. Amelia walked over to Frederick and said, "This is it! Is everything set?" Frederick folded his arms and shrugged. "Obviously, don't you trust me?" he asked. Patrick walked over to Frederick only to realize Amelia was there; he recognized the back of her head. She turned around and made eye contact with him, then scurried away. "Is everything all set?" Patrick asked. "Be there at midnight. You know the drill," Frederick replied.

Chapter 27: Midnight

Amelia, Frederick, Dylan, Patrick and the rest of the dancers were freaking out backstage. The stage was bright, the music started, and the sky was dark. It had been an hour since the tiny snow flurries started falling. There were hundreds of camera crews and reporters. There were so many thousands of people the crowd was in gridlock pattern in front of the stage. People in the crowd were dressed in mittens, hats, earmuffs, coats and boats; yet still shivering and blowing out cold air as they cheered. The crowd was roaring and clapping. There wasn't one frown in the sea of faces.

Charisse came over to the dancers and warned them "you guys are up next. The second you hear our song, the lights will go out, you hurry onto the stage and get to your places. You guys got this. Let's say a little prayer together first," she said. Within five minutes, they were all on stage. Kelly and her family were in the third row back, with a sign *"We love you, Patrick!" that* he saw once the lights were turned on and shined into the crowd briefly.

All their work and practice came to fruition that evening. The music was loud, the crowd was happy, and the dancers were proud as they finished the show. They came back on the stage for a final bow together at the end of the show. "Let's all go watch the fireworks together, it's almost midnight!" Charisse shouted. The group walked to the East River and waited for the fireworks. Their families came with them. Frederick's father, Patrick's father, and Dylan's father got along well and bonded over how proud they were of their sons. Kelly came over and whispered in Patrick's ear, "I can't wait!"

"5,4,3,2,1, HAPPY NEW YEAR!" everyone shouted. Frederick turned to Dylan and said, "I love you!" and Dylan kissed him in return. The fireworks belted out and lit up the sky. "I LOVE YOU AMELIA" was written across the sky in purple, red, and blue. Everyone pointed in amazement. Frederick high fived his father. Amelia stood there in awe. Patrick took her by the hand, pulled her in, and passionately kissed her. Kelly gave a thumbs up in the background.

The show was not over. Everyone in the group gasped when a red and white horse drawn carriage pulled up to them. The driver stopped, and Professor Bryant came out. He got down on one knee and said, "Charisse, please be my wife," She jumped up and screamed, "YES!" at the top of her lungs. She hopped in the carriage, and they were off.

Amelia knew it wasn't a good time to tell Charisse, so she put the records in Charisse's mailbox the next day as she walked around the city. On January 2nd, she received a phone call. It was Charisse. "I don't know what to say. I donated my eggs so many years ago and never looked back," Charisse explained.

"You don't have to explain. The show is over. I understand if you don't want to have anymore contact with me," Amelia replied. "No, not at all. I know I can never replace your mother, but can we get a green tea sometime?" Charisse sincerely asked. "I would love to," said Amelia. "Mocha Lattes," Charisse suggested. "You know me too well," Amelia replied. "Whoever said dancing genes don't run in families?" Charisse laughed. And just like that, their first mother-daughter meeting was set.

www.ingramcontent.com/pod-product-compliance
Lightning Source LLC
Chambersburg PA
CBHW070747160726
48004CB00001B/84